Praise for *The Son of Man*
Finalist for the Cercador Pr
Winner of the Prix du Roman
Longlisted for the Prix Femina

"A striking aspect of this macabre, mythlike story is its linguistic extravagance." —*Wall Street Journal*

"Even the most faithfully translated books can lack a vital spark of the original. But in Frank Wynne's translation of an exquisite 2021 novel by French wunderkind Jean-Baptiste Del Amo, the story—an atmospheric exploration of filial relationships—loses none of its taut beauty." —*Bloomberg*

"Dark, uncompromising, and poetic . . . Del Amo has crafted a work imbued less with a sense of dread, and more with a sense of inevitability . . . Both an excoriation of toxic masculinity, and a plea for understanding . . . Powerful, moving, and thought-provoking." —*GLAM Adelaide*

"A brooding, brutal pastoral . . . Inexorable, bleak, and ugly, but it's hard to look away." —*NZ Herald Listener*

"Del Amo follows up his memorable *Animalia* with another arresting French rural gothic . . . Del Amo's signature florid style comes to life in Wynne's consummate translation, and at the heart of the lurid plot is a sensitive depiction of a boy's confusion. Once this gets its hooks in readers, it won't let go." —*Publishers Weekly*

"Serene descriptions of the surrounding forest and its dazzling plant and animal life contrasts with unflinching descriptions of gunshot wounds and the father's brutal behavior. The result is an intense French gothic drama that one knows from the outset cannot end happily." —*Booklist*

"*The Son of Man* is a complete vision: a parable as palpable as the flesh Del Amo renders in painstaking detail. Dread and horror and beauty all at once—this book defies categorization. I loved every carefully crafted sentence, even as I feared what the next page would bring." —Garrard Conley, author of *All the World Beside*

"*The Son of Man* is an explosion, a shout. Jean-Baptiste Del Amo is a storming talent; here are words which are forged rather than written, smeared with blood."
—**Daisy Johnson, author of *Sisters***

"An exquisite and mesmerizing novel, in which violence constantly threatens to break the surface. The precision and detail of the prose imprints on the mind like a photograph."
—**Isabella Hammad, author of *Enter Ghost***

"*The Son of Man* is an astonishing book. Beautifully written, devastating at times, and relentless, but unforgettable."
—**Michael Magee, author of *Close to Home***

"A novel of mounting tension, of violence handed down through generations of men like a terrible heirloom. Jean-Baptiste Del Amo is a master of horrific landscapes, landscapes which are rendered horrific by and through the humans who live in them. I would follow him into any deep, dark forest."
—**Madeleine Watts, author of *The Inland Sea***

"*The Son of Man* demands a fearless kind of reading. It combines the impassive eye of a naturalist regarding their object of study, with the fierce revolt of that which is scrutinized, and resists being catalogued and known. Del Amo reaches into atavistic territories of impulse, desire, violence and repetition, and refuses to domesticate through conclusion. I was mesmerized by this formidable tale of a son and a mother who come up against both the law of the father and the lawlessness of nature."
—**Daisy Lafarge, author of *Paul***

"In [*The Son of Man*] the simple plot becomes as complex as the psychology of these human beasts. The writing is never precious, always precise. As the tension mounts, the sentences become longer and meandering, elusive like erupting violence. Rarely has the 39-year-old author hit the right notes so perfectly in the way he stretches his fiction."
—*Le Monde*

"Jean-Baptiste Del Amo constructs a mythology that is both familial and pantheistic to describe a child's discovery of the cruelty of the adult world. He writes with an absolute exactitude, the scenes of the novel are instantly visual and the exploration of feelings is allied to the precision of the descriptions. By placing itself on the side of the child whilst sticking to the third person, the novel goes deep into the boys' feelings, depicts the fusional relationship with a loving mother, the distant relationship with a father who appears out of nowhere and with whom the child craves a strong union, the discovery of the brutality of the world of adults and the truly physical bond with nature and animals ... [*The Son of Man*] is a deep and subtle novel. —*Télérama*

"The theme of transmission between father and son is at the heart of the novel. It is marked by a macabre determinism, everything is already played for, poisoned. A wandering insane grandfather casts a shadow and bad luck ricochets on his descendants. Jean-Baptiste Del Amo does not shy away from showing the atrocious. He has several strings to his hunter's bow; an art of careful framing, of scenic observation. A taste for the primeval drive mixed with intuitions and perceptions ... Brief moments of light amidst the darkness and a fear so intense you could cut it with a knife." —*Le Figaro Littéraire*

"With [*The Son of Man*], Jean-Baptiste Del Amo focuses intensely on the imperceptible tipping point in violence. The reader gets beyond a horror reminiscent of *The Shining* in this *huis clos* with an open sky, this is fiction lifted by a highly powerful elliptic structure and one suffocates in the middle of nature, aware of intentions that can be guessed without ever being openly expressed." —*Elle Magazine*

"Jean-Baptiste Del Amo signs here a story of rare power that does not let go of the reader until the last page, the writing is dazzling. One of the most brilliant authors of his generation." —*RTL (radio)*

"Jean-Baptiste Del Amo gives a soul to this drama. We oscillate constantly between nature writing, a tale and a psychological novel. The writing is sumptuously lyrical, organic and describes with intensity the many ways in which life is derailed." —*Livres Hebdo*

"Five years after [*Animalia*], Jean-Baptiste Del Amo continues his exploration of violence and transmission and this *huis clos* first suffocating, then toxic and dangerous." —*Les Inrockuptibles*

ALSO BY JEAN-BAPTISTE DEL AMO

Animalia

Jean-Baptiste Del Amo

The SON of MAN

Translated from the French by
FRANK WYNNE

Grove Press
New York

Copyright © 2021 by Éditions Gallimard
Translation copyright © 2024 by Frank Wynne

All rights reserved. No part of this book may be reproduced in any form or by any electronic or mechanical means, including information storage and retrieval systems, without permission in writing from the publisher, except by a reviewer, who may quote brief passages in a review. Scanning, uploading, and electronic distribution of this book or the facilitation of such without the permission of the publisher is prohibited. Please purchase only authorized electronic editions, and do not participate in or encourage electronic piracy of copyrighted materials. Your support of the author's rights is appreciated. Any member of educational institutions wishing to photocopy part or all of the work for classroom use, or anthology, should send inquiries to Grove Atlantic, 154 West 14th Street, New York, NY 10011 or permissions@groveatlantic.com.

Any use of this publication to train generative artificial intelligence ("AI") technologies is expressly prohibited. The author and publisher reserve all rights to license uses of this work for generative AI training and development of machine learning language models.

First published in 2021 as *Le fils de l'homme*.
First published in English in 2024 in Great Britain
by Fitzcarraldo Editions.

Printed in the United States of America

This book was set in 11.75-pt. Minion Pro
by Alpha Design & Composition of Pittsfield, NH.

First Grove Atlantic hardcover edition: July 2024
First Grove Atlantic paperback edition: July 2025

ISBN 978-0-8021-6499-5
eISBN 978-0-8021-6091-1

Library of Congress Cataloging-in-Publication data is available for this title.

Grove Press
an imprint of Grove Atlantic
154 West 14th Street
New York, NY 10011

Distributed by Publishers Group West

groveatlantic.com

25 26 27 28   10 9 8 7 6 5 4 3 2 1

"Let the feverish rage of fathers live on in sons through every generation."

—Seneca, *Thyestes*

The leader stops, looks up at the sky and, for an instant, the black disc of his pupil aligns with the white disc of the sun, the star sears the retina and the creature crawling through the matricial mud turns away to contemplate the valley through which he is trudging with others of his kind: a landscape whipped by winds, sparse undergrowth dotted here and there with shrubs that have a mournful air; over this bleak terrain floats the negative afterimage of the day star, a black moon suspended on the horizon.

For days now, they have been marching westward, into the biting autumn wind. Thick, unkempt beards erode the hard features of the men. Ruddy-faced women carry newborns in tattered pelts. Many will die along the way, from the blue bitter cold or from dysentery contracted from stagnant watering holes where the feral herds come to drink. For them the men, with their gnarled fingers or their blades, will dig desolate hollows in the earth.

Into these pits they will place the shrouded bodies, more piteous still in the darkness of the grave; they will drop in useless trinkets, the fur in which the child would nestle, a doll of plaited hemp, a necklet of bones that will soon be indistinguishable from those of the dead child. Onto the lifeless face they will toss fistfuls of earth that seal up the eyes, the mouth, then they will place heavy rocks upon the burial mound to protect the remains from carrion feeders scavenging for sustenance. At length, they will set off once more, and only the mother will perhaps give a last glance over her shoulder at the glittering pile of stones quickly consumed by the shadow cast by the hill.

An old man drags his emaciated body beneath a thick pelt whose fleece moves with each gust of wind. Time was, he led the group through plains and valleys, along the banks of waterways towards more nourishing earth, more clement skies. Now, he struggles to follow those younger and more robust than he, those who walk ahead, who decide where to pitch camp at dusk and strike camp at daybreak. Sometimes, at the mouth of a cave where they break their journey, they may light a fire that slashes the darkness, its flames illumining sketches of creatures that others before them have daubed onto the walls by the flickering glow of a tallow lamp.

In the crushing darkness, they huddle together, their rude bodies buried beneath great pelts from which only their faces emerge. Their breath condenses, their eyes remain open, while mothers attempt to soothe their babes, brushing a breast against their lips. Some of the men talk in low voices, stir up the embers which blaze and send out sparks whose reflections orbit the irises of those keeping watch and soar and whirl as though they would rejoin the firmament where other stars gutter out and die, engulfed by the ravening heart of night.

The enforced closeness beneath the covering pelts enjoins them to couple. Sometimes ignoring the child she is warming against her belly, the male will seize the rump that the female offers or listlessly denies him, and, taking the sex he has lubricated with a thick gob of spittle, will thrust until he comes inside her. Before *trickling down her thigh as she drifts off again, the seed may fecundate the female, who, three seasons later, biting down on a piece of wood, will be delivered in the shadow of a hedgerow, a few steps from the camp the group has pitched to allow for the birthing.*

Crouching on the ground, her arms gripped by other women who sponge her brow in turn, her calves, her sex, she will expel the fruit of this siring onto the bare earth, or into the hands of a midwife. The umbilical cord will be cut with a sharp flint. The thing thus dragged into the light and laid upon the empty skin of the belly will crawl in order to drink colostrum from the teat, thereby initiating the cycle necessary to its survival that will see it tirelessly ingurgitate the world and excrete it.

If the child survives the first summers and the first winters, if his remains do not go to join all those they have already lost along the way – of one of these, snatched by a marten and carried to a nearby pool, there remains only the ribcage, half-buried in the mud where, beneath the vault of ribs that will soon crumble to dust, a bone-white sprig of common horsetail rises – he will soon walk beside others of his kind, be welcomed among them, learn to read the map of the stars, to strike flints to produce fire or fashion knives, learn the secrets of plants, bind up wounds and ready the bodies of the dead for their ultimate journey.

Perhaps the child will know a reprieve, survive to reach the fateful hour when his already weary flesh issues the order to reproduce. At this, he will tirelessly seek to mate with another of his kind, blindly fumbling and groping another of the miserable creatures in the cold of the blazing darkness, as the Milky

Way punctures the sky above their heads. Then, having trodden the earth awhile, having known a handful of pallid dawns and twilights, the searing intensity of childhood and the body's inexorable decay, he will die in some fashion or other before he has attained the age of thirty.

But, for now, the child still belongs to oblivion; he is but a minuscule, incongruous probability as the horde of humans advance, heads bowed against the windstorm, an upright, stubborn, tatterdemalion herd. Upon their shoulders or on sleds they carry tanned hides and earthenware pots fashioned by their own hands containing stores of fat. In these they preserve the roots, nuts and berries gathered along the way on which they feed, chewing the shrivelled flesh, the fibre rendered edible by fat, sucking out the juices sweet or bitter.

After a trek of many weeks, they come to the bank of a river teeming with fish, whose sinuous bed unfurls as far as the eye can see across the plain stalked by the shadows of the clouds that scud from east to west. The shadows race ahead, cloaking vast stretches of land in darkness, deepening the hollows, levelling the peat bogs, adding a density to the forests that turns their greenish-brown to carbon black and transforming the stagnant waters of the marsh into vast sheets of glass bristling with reeds that rustle in the wind like insect wings. The clouds wreathing the pristine peaks move on, light bursts through again and sets the earth ablaze. A glean of herons rises from the marshes; the arrow of their necks cleaves the air, the furled wings shimmering against the electric blue.

* * *

The humans stop and pitch camp. Some who are skilled fishermen wade into the current that foams around boulders and the tree trunks carried here by floodwaters. The fishermen move along the banks, peering into the depths. The surface reflects their ape-like faces and, beyond, the nebulous sky floating above the dappled pebbles worn smooth by the river. The roar of the torrent and the effort required to see through the surging, shimmering water quickly plunge the fishermen into a kind of trance. Bodies bowed, arms hanging by their sides, the roiling water rising to thighs or waists, their hands lightly skimming the surface, they advance, like dusky wading birds formed by the river.

One of them bends lower and plunges his arm into the current. In a pool of calm water, near a tree trunk lying partly on the bank, the fisherman has spotted the ghostly form of a salmon swimming against the current, its steely reflections merging with the constantly shifting waters of the stream. With infinite slowness, he moves closer, ensuring that his shadow does not go before him. He lets his arms dangle just below the surface, which so distorts his vision that his hands look as though they are no longer part of the fisherman, but belong to the hermetic world of the river – and he stares fixedly at the salmon's eye, the iris speckled with gold, the opalescent periorbital scales.

With boundless caution, the fisherman brings his hands together beneath the salmon's belly and, for an instant, it looks as though he is holding a sacrifice, that he is offering the salmon to the river, or that he is buoying it up in its precious delicate stasis. As his palms brush against the pelvic fins, the fish starts and swerves, though makes no attempt to escape. The fisherman waits, motionless; his palms now holding nothing but shifting flashes of light. Once again, he moves his hands so that they are under the salmon; this time the fish allows him to stroke its belly, even lift it, and it is only as its dorsal fin breaks the surface of the water that it violently twists and turns in an effort to escape.

But the fisherman's hands have closed around it; with a powerful flick, he lifts the fish out of the water and tosses it into the air towards the bank, where a number of children are waiting, armed with hazel wands whose ends have been sharpened to a point. One of them, a hirsute little girl who is blind in one eye, rushes towards the salmon, which is floundering on the gravel. Crouching down, she holds it still with one hand and thrusts the pointed stick through its gills until it emerges from its mouth. Vainly it opens and closes its lower jaw, as the little girl holds the impaled fish at arm's length, its body gleaming in the sunlight.

Hunkered on the gravel bank, the women gut the salmon caught by the fishermen. The dark skin of their hands is spangled with fish scales as they insert a sharpened flint into the anus, make an incision along the abdomen, hook their index and middle fingers into the opening to clean out the cavity. They pull out a small pile of reddish-brown entrails which they toss onto the ground with a flick of the wrist. The little one-eyed girl standing near them is watching intently. From between two stones, she picks up a swim bladder, gazes for a moment at its iridescent whiteness, then bursts it between her fingers.

From a framework of branches, the women suspend an animal hide which they fill with water and large pebbles that they have heated in the glowing embers of the fire. To this, they add freshwater mussels collected by the children, some tubers, herbs that were gathered and dried the previous summer, and lastly the fish whose flesh quickly begins to flake. Before long, the fragrant steam from the bubbling broth pervades the placid, blue-tinged riverbank.

At night, they eat their fill, and the youngest, exhausted by the long walk and their frantic games in the rushing waters, fall asleep around the fire to the sound of an incantation sung by the former leader. It is a song that predates song, that predates voice itself, a guttural cadenced lament composed of dissonant modulations and vibrato, deep booming exhalations in which the old man's body serves as a resonance chamber. At times it seems that secrets from the deepest night, from the invisible plain, from the black riverbed and the very heart of the stones issue forth, not from the old man, but from somewhere beyond him – secrets summoned by this body as dry and gnarled as a tree stump, for in that grizzled face nothing moves or flickers save the luminous orb of flames.

The lips barely move beneath the beard, the eyes are closed, the gaze turned inward. The threnody brings with it a torrent of images, of sensations, and deep within their flesh, all gathered here feel a profound melancholy, one that speaks of their wanderings over the earth, aimless and devoid of all meaning, of the endless cycle of the seasons, of the dead who continue to travel by their sides and are conjured in the anteroom of night by a furtive shadow or the howl of a wolf. And when the old man falls silent, when the chant within him dwindles, they hold their breath; something of their insignificance and their majesty has been expressed.

In the wan light of morning, the world unveils itself, glittering in its winter shroud. Their men's breath condenses in the icy air as they rekindle the fire. Here and there, they have dug holes and stretched hides between tall posts, erecting a few huts beneath which the women and children are sleeping still, huddled together beneath other hides.

Jackdaws wheel above the camp, perch on the branches of a tree a short distance away, their jet-black plumage silhouetted against the hoarfrost that has settled on the bark. They watch these men who might well discard something they can eat; the men watch the jackdaws knowing that, from time to time, they might lead them to carrion, circling and squabbling over a carcass that the men can steal and bring back to camp and eat.

Before long, their reserves run out. They feed on nuts, on acorns that they crush and boil again and again to remove the tannins before moulding them into biscuits and cooking them over coals. They dig into dead tree trunks in search of larvae, pull up the roots, peel away the edible bark and mosses.

At the dawn of a new day, they see a herd of deer grazing on the edge of a forest. They arm themselves with spears whose shafts of stripped pine are armed with shards of flint and fletchings of falcon or barn owl feathers. They set off in utter silence: a woman and three men. Behind the last of them tails a gaunt-faced boy who looks barely pubescent. His limbs are scrawny, his movements awkward, downy hair covers his cheeks and upper lip. He looks in wonderment from hunter to hunter with dark eyes that are deeply sunken in sockets chiselled beneath the prominent brow ridge. He shoots glances at the man bringing up the rear – his genitor – whom he follows closely. He tries to understand the hunters' movements, and consciously emulates their stillness.

At first the party seems to veer away from the calmly grazing deer – one of them, a roebuck that shed his antlers last autumn, raises his head and looks around, stiffens, sniffs the air, exhales, the white cloud of his breath hovering over his head as though he has just brought forth his soul – moving in a wide arc heading west, through the brushwood where night still lingers, their silhouettes barely visible as the moon pales and sets while dawn, a sudden pink and purple, comes and splits heaven from earth.

The hunters stand stock still as the roebuck surveys the terrain and move on only when the animal lowers his head. As they wait amid the tall, bleached grass, the adolescent sees his father take a leather pouch from beneath the tangled hides he wears. He lifts it up and, pressing with his fingers, produces a small cloud of ash that drifts towards their huddled bodies as it disperses, indicating that a gentle breeze is blowing in their direction.

The father nods and the hunters set off once more. They reach the edge of the forest and step into its shadows just as, in the east, the great fire rises, spilling its fulvous light across the plain.

The hunters advance, careful as to where they place their feet on the bed of leaves and twigs covered with frost. Soon, they have a more detailed view of the herd which comprises the roebuck, three does and a male kid, doubtless born in spring since already he has an adult's slate-grey coat, beaded with dew. The pale gorget patches at the base of their throats are visible when they raise their heads; their white lower lips sharply contrast with their deep black muzzles, and they have pale oval patches on their rumps.

With rapid hand gestures, the father signals for the other two hunters to skirt around the herd and head off. The boy watches as they disappear, engulfed by the shadowy trunks, the blackness of the forest. The man lays a hand on his shoulder and directs him to a fallen tree. Together, they hunker out of sight and survey the grassland, the drifting patches of fog, the distant smoke of the camp, the deer framed against the light of the rising star, the mass of their bodies reduced to a silhouette while the contours are blurred by the light such that they look fragile, insubstantial, as though at any moment they might dissolve.

Their bodies ache from the cold and their crouched position. In their fists, they grip their spear shafts. The eyes of the son never leave his father's face. From the distance comes a sound, like the shrill cry of some bird of prey; the man slots his spear into the bow, the son emulates his actions. They hold their breath until the grassland is pierced by a second cry. They watch as the deer suddenly bound, leave off grazing and run straight towards them. The two beaters burst from the undergrowth and race towards the herd, spreading out as they advance.

Led by the roebuck, the bevy attempts to break for the wide expanse of grassland, but the female hunter moves to block their path. Bringing a hand up to his chest, the father signals to his son to stay motionless. The son watches as the deer bound towards them in a silence broken only by their exhalations and the muffled thud of hooves between each majestic leap.

The father lowers his hand and, as one man, father and son stand, surging from behind the fallen tree. They see the roebuck's head jerk back. Its eye wide with fear, the animal deploys the whole weight of its body to wheel around and head towards the undergrowth.

In that instant, all the hunters launch their spears, which rise into the pale morning. Everything is suspended; their weapons tracing their arc over the plains, the deer hovering above tufts of grasses, the roebuck's muzzle almost touching the shadow beneath the trees where dead leaves continue to spiral down even as the boughs begin to bud, the dark mass of the humans pursuing them and, farther off, a flight of white birds flushed from a thicket by the bolting deer.

The spears simultaneously launched by the father and the female hunter come to earth in the wake of the fleeing deer, the sonorous thud quivering through the long shafts. The one thrown by the second beater glides into the long grass with the hiss of a snake, while the spear thrown by the adolescent soundlessly embeds itself into the shoulder of one of the does.

The animal lists to the right, collapses onto its forelegs in the bed of leaves and frost-covered branches which crack beneath its weight. In a convulsive spasm that shakes the deer's whole body, it manages to get to its feet and, with a leap, disappears into the forest. The hunters gather up their weapons and plunge into the forest in pursuit of the herd, but already the roe deers' coats have merged with the infinite procession of tree trunks; only the pale oval patches on their rumps make it possible to follow their fitful leaps into the tall ferns scorched by the cold. Once again, the hunters spread out as they begin a second advance, their progress hindered by the dense undergrowth and the sweet-smelling peat bogs.

Beneath the trees, everything is bathed in a cold light that flattens shapes and leaches colours. When the father bends down and presses his hand against a powdery tree trunk, the blood that stains his fingertips is strangely dark; he has to thrust his arm into a well of daylight formed by the bare branches of a beech before the stain reveals itself as startling crimson. Wiping his fingers on the hide that covers his chest, he studies the forest floor and, in a patch of bog, discovers hoofprints of the stricken doe that clearly indicate that she is limping and can no longer put her weight on her left foreleg.

The hammering of a woodpecker against a hollow trunk is heard at regular intervals. A bough falls onto a bed of leaves with a muted crunch. Farther off, unseen by his father, the adolescent is looking up into dark treetops. Over him, his breath clouds and dissipates. He studies the knotted tangle of vegetation they must conquer in order to advance, the glistening trunks, the sinuous snarl of roots that emerge from the humus. The intoxicating forest smell leaves him disoriented. He is no longer aware of the presence of the other hunters. He feels as though the forest has propelled him into its vegetal depths, that murky, mucilaginous terrain where it produces its secret fermentations.

Leaning against the sodden bark of trees, he extracts his foot from water-logged holes, from tangles of liana, from the vast putrefaction that feeds the earth and that, come spring, will cause relentless life once more to burst forth from its womb. Mute daylight shimmers beyond the trees.

Walking on, he comes to a clearing strewn with winter heather. The wounded doe is lying amid the shrubs dotted with purple flowers. Turning her head, she licks the flank that is pierced by a spear whose shaft now rests on the ground. The adolescent stays out of sight, hidden by the trees. He watches the young roebuck fretfully trot back and forth along the edge of the forest. The doe leaves off licking her flank and looks up at the kid. Resting her weight on her hind legs, she attempts to stand upright but manages only to raise her rump before falling again heavily. Stretching out her neck, she lays her head on the ground and does not lift it when the young hunter emerges from his hide. A brief shudder courses through her body at the idea that she could flee; meanwhile the kid darts into the cover of the trees and stands there, motionless.

The adolescent walks over to the doe, stands next to her, his shadow falling on the chest and flank that rises and falls with her rapid, ragged breathing. He breathes in the sweet smell of game and the ferrous tang of blood that mats her coat. He senses the beating of the heart beneath the visible arc of the ribs. The eye, with its oval pupil at the centre of a brown iris, offers a distorted reflection of the world, the young hunter, the convex lines of the pines with their coppery trunks, the vaulted sky above the treetops. From it flows a translucent liquid that clings to the lashes and darkens the short hair of the cheeks. There is the sound of footsteps from the undergrowth. The young hunter turns his head and sees the shadow of his father approaching through the trees.

He turns back to the roebuck, still watching warily from the half-light of the trees, he bends, pulls a half-buried rock from the ground and hurls it towards the animal with all his strength. The projectile hits a tree trunk, the young roebuck lopes off, pauses to take a last look at the clearing and the prostrate doe, then, with a bound, he vanishes.

The father bursts into the clearing and lumbers over to the son, gripping the shaft of his spear. When he reaches the young hunter, he looks down at the doe, then, cupping his hands around his mouth, he lets out a brief repeated sound that rises in the quavering air. As the man crouches next to her, the doe lets out a husky breath. The sun has just soared above the treetops and now bathes all three – the man, the child, the doe – with a blazing light that causes steam to rise from their dew-covered skin. The other two hunters emerge from the forest and walk towards them.

The father sets his weapon down on the heather, lays his left hand on the deer's shoulder and grips the shaft of the spear thrown by the boy. His hand slides up the polished wood to get a higher grip. Then, with a forceful thrust that causes every tendon in his neck to bulge, he drives it into the animal's chest. The sharpened flint cuts a path through the complex network of muscles, nerves and blood vessels, pierces the heart of the doe, whose body is racked by a single shudder which is held in check by the hunter's hand pressing on its shoulder. With a jerk of equal force, the hunter removes the spear. The shaft and the head fly out; crimson blood runs down the deer's flank and drips onto the ground.

The father thrusts his hand into the open wound in the doe's flank, gets to his feet and daubs a vertical red line on the young hunter's cheek. Then he lays his hand against the child's face, grubby thumb pressed against the cheekbone, fingers resting beneath his ear. He lingers for an instant, in a caress that leaves the boy's skin prickling with the sensation of the cold, calloused hand long after it is withdrawn.

Grabbing the doe's legs, the father lifts the carcass off the ground and hoists it onto his shoulders. The animal's neck rests against his arm; the eye is dull and veiled, it no longer reflects anything, while the wound continues to trickle blood. As the father sets off through the forest, heading back to the camp, the deer's head lolling against his arm, the other hunters follow. The child stands, motionless, in the middle of the clearing. He gazes up at a falcon as it hovers, his face flooded with light. When he returns his attention to his own kind, he sees the female hunter stop and glance back at him before leaving the forest. He is alone now in the hushed heart of the wood. The birds have fallen silent. He seems to consider staying here, amid the winter heather, the murmur of the trees, and abandoning the group. He would lie down in the still-warm hollow left by the body of the doe and, staring up into the sky, let himself be buried beneath the dead leaves, the fertile humus.

The falcon lets out a shrill cry and swoops down on a small beast of prey somewhere on the grasslands. Then, the young hunter bends down and picks up his spear.

IN THE EARLY HOURS of morning, they leave the town behind them.

In the back seat of the battered old estate car, the son is dozing. Through half-closed eyes he looks out of the window at the succession of suburban houses, an industrial estate, and the floodlights that spill into the night.

They pass the former goods station, the freight cars cloaked in rust and darkness, beached among the brambles, the silos of a farmers' cooperative haloed in a mist that glows blue in the beam of the spotlight trained on the huge concrete slab suddenly crossed by a raw-boned dog.

The child watches the animal disappear into the shadow of a dump truck. He drifts off and the dog reappears in dreams punctuated by the lights that pulse through the window. The dog is trotting along beside him on a path somewhere deep in the forest – unless it is a tranquil, untamed prairie, he cannot tell. His hand brushes the dog's head, he rests his palm there. The two are walking at the same pace, their breathing perfectly in sync, and now they are a single creature, the bodies of animal and child fused into one, launched into the boundless night, the infinite space that opens up before them.

The mother glances up, looking at him in the rearview mirror. Even in sleep, he feels the familiar balm of her brown eyes on him. Often he has lain down on his mother's bed, the two of them curled up facing each other, heads resting on their folded arms, and in the coolness of the bedroom ablaze with light, he has studied his mother's face, her eyes, marked by something inexpressible, an infinite sadness or a resignation, as though, face to face with her son, she found herself helpless and ashamed.

In the distance, a fire smoulders beneath the starless sky, a dragon's breath, or an oil refinery. The mother stares at it for a moment before it disappears behind a line of barren trees, then she glances at the father who stares at the road, impassive and unblinking, his left hand gripping the steering wheel. Only the muscle in his jaw tenses from time to time beneath the skin of a cheek darkened by a stubbly beard.

Later, they stop at a service station and the child is woken by the slam of doors.

'Pass me a cigarette, could you?' the mother asks.

The father nods to the glove compartment and walks around the car. Through the back window, the son sees the clouds of breath in the crackling glow of a neon light. The gauge whirls as the humming petrol pump fills up the car's belly.

The mother has wandered away from the car, tugging the collar of her parka. She lights a cigarette, exhales a first plume of smoke – she holds the filter between the distal phalanges of her index and middle fingers, close to the nails – walks down the central reservation of yellowed grass, then retraces her steps. She brings the cigarette to her lips, darting brief glances that linger on the shadows nesting in the branches of trees and in privet hedges.

The child opens the car door, gets out and breathes in the smell of diesel. He stretches, walks towards his mother, who, seeing him, tosses the cigarette butt on the ground and crushes it with the sole of her shoe. As it falls, the butt traces an arabesque of tiny embers that blaze more brightly as they are consumed. The boy comes and huddles against her.

They do not speak, dimly illuminated by the light from the petrol station, which, in the fog, looks like a ghost ship from the merchant navy. The child inhales the perfume of detergent and tobacco from her parka. The mother runs her hand over the child's red hair, lingers at the nape of his neck.

'Time to go,' says the father.

She nods and her hand slides from her son's neck to his cheek.

'Are we nearly there yet?' the child asks.

'I don't know,' she says. 'A few more hours.'

They get back into the car and set off again. Before long, as they drive along the main road, there is nothing but the darkness that is slashed by the beams of the headlights only to instantly close up over them. Patches of fog appear, pale spectres that hover above the tarmac and are slain by the car and devoured by the night.

They drive through a valley glimpsed only in fragments by the light of the headlamps: coniferous forests, hedges of barbed acacias guarding barely visible meadows blanketed with frost, hulking farmhouses of freestone with slate roofs, sometimes huddled together in small hamlets where the buildings are so close-set they seem like blockhouses or the last remnants of a lost civilization.

As the valley closes in, sleeping colossi rise up before them, limestone crags whose summits are invisible, dark looming shadows more impenetrable than night; it feels as though the car is hurtling towards an impassable wall that could only have been built by a god.

The car hurtles into a tunnel, and the beams of the headlights are swept up so that they reflect off the brute concrete curves and back into the car as a yellowish radiance that outlines the faces of the father and the mother. Above their heads, the unimaginable mass of mountain flashes past, tens of thousands of tonnes of igneous rock, layer upon layer of granite, quartz, mica and sedimentary rock. The child lying on the back seat holds his breath, wondering how the tunnel can hold up such a weight by itself. Could the mountain suddenly collapse and bury them alive?

As they emerge into another valley, the halo of the headlights hits a wall of dense fog that forces the father to slow down.

Road signs briefly appear – beacons in this becalmed sea – a roundabout, a string of identical villages with dark, vertiginous streets, reduplicated village squares next to identical churches flanked by plane trees with branches marbled by pigeon droppings, the churches, sinister and solemn as dolmens, each with its gothic arch and the steeple piercing the darkness.

In turn, the villages disappear and the car heads up a winding road of hairpin bends, past unexpected fields in the middle of which are dozing herds that cling to the stony ground, large bales of hay, some piled beneath tarpaulins, others carelessly abandoned next to a feeder or an old enamel bathtub that serves as a drinking trough, the ties broken, the hay bale sagging and sodden; here and there are other buildings, new-build houses, dairy farms or one-time sheepfolds built against the slopes, fashioned from the mountain itself, with pale rubblestone, mossy roofs and windows as wide and gaping as chasms.

Along the road, the child sees a wayside cross supporting a pallid Christ cast from metal, his body covered with patches of lichen or rust. The last wisps of fog suddenly dissolve and the hard lines of the massif emerge. The darkness now carries within it the promise of dawn, that almost imperceptible shift that frames the contours of the world that cannot yet be grasped, offering only varying degrees of darkness. A veil that was invisible until that moment rends itself; all the things that were cloaked in the wings of night are suddenly bathed in a bluish glow that does not seem to come from without, but to emanate from within them, a silvery phosphorescence leaching from the rocks, the asphalt, the trunks of the pines and the foliage.

The father turns the car onto a dirt track that disappears into a small valley thick with beech trees, sessile oaks and conifers. A little stream snakes silently below, dark water ripples around the rocks that break the surface and, in the unmoving undergrowth, something else is in suspense, a quivering impatience; night withdraws, creating vast shadowy hollows beneath the branches of the trees where clouds of birds twitch and chirrup.

'Shit,' says the father, stamping on the brake.

Straight ahead, a pine trunk looms in the glare of the headlights. He opens his door and gets out of the car.

'What's the matter?' says the child.

'A tree fell across the road,' says the mother.

They watch as the father inspects the fallen trunk, places one foot on the glistening bark and pushes with all his might, but the topmost branches of the pine are caught between two oaks on the other side of the path. He comes back to the car and slides in behind the steering wheel.

'We can't go any further. I don't have a saw to cut it up.'

'Couldn't the two of us shift it together?'

'No way. It's not completely uprooted. We'll have to go the rest of the way on foot.'

The father steers the car onto the embankment, the tyres spinning on the loose ground sending up showers of dirt and gravel, then a sudden swerve sends the car hurtling into a dark clearing filled with ferns. The father pulls up the handbrake, shifts down into first gear and shuts off the ignition.

'Gather the stuff,' he says.

All three get out of the car.

The father opens the boot, takes out a rucksack and hands it to the mother. She takes it and, with some difficulty, carries it down to the path and sets it at her feet.

To the son, the father hands a second backpack which is smaller, though clearly too heavy – at least for the frail frame of a nine-year-old boy – since when the father gestures for him to turn around and helps him put his arms through the straps, the boy grunts and stoops under the weight before warily picking his way down the embankment to join his mother.

From the boot, the father hauls the last of the bags; it is much bigger than the others, a military-style haversack with numerous straps and pockets, and the father grimaces as he carries it as far as the fallen trunk and props it up there.

Then he goes back to the car, rummages around until he finds a camouflage net and a flashlight. He checks the battery. A wide beam of light cuts through the gloomy clearing, illuminating the countless trees and the steep slope.

The father slams the doors of the estate, activates the central locking, slips the handle of the flashlight into his back pocket of his jeans. He unfolds the camouflage netting, spreads it over the car and studies the surrounding area.

He takes a few steps, trampling the brown mass of ferns and the dense soil from which they draw sustenance and, from around the foot of the trees, frees some old fallen boughs half-buried by moss and liana. Some are so rotten that they crumble as he pulls them towards him, others emerge from the humus to reveal branchlets that make it seem as though he is uprooting huge ligneous plants.

The father drags them to the vehicle and carefully lays them at an angle so that the car can barely be seen from the road.

Mother and son watch from the bottom of the slope. The father searches around until he finds two rocks which he places beneath the rear tyres, kicking them into place. Heaving the military kitbag onto his back, he heads back down to the path, then turns and spends a moment looking at how the camouflage netting and the branches blend the car into the shadows.

The father snuffles, wipes his nose with the back of his hands and says:

'Let's go.'

* * *

He sets off walking, the mother and son follow behind. The boy glances around at the hushed undergrowth where nothing rustles, nothing moves. He becomes aware of the smell of the mountain, a pungent scent composed of rotting vegetation, barks, bracket fungi and mosses swollen with rainwater, of the invertebrate creatures that stealthily crawl beneath the ancient trunks and the powdery rocks of the riverbed.

With every step, the boy breathes in this scent that overwhelms and leaves him so light-headed that he has to make a considerable effort to focus on the relentless cadence of the father's soles as they pound the stony ground, so that he does not lose the rhythm of the march despite his dizziness.

The path curves eastward across the north face of the mountain while, to their left, a gap in the serried trees reveals a patch of sky slashed by the dawn which frames the limestone dolomites and the sheer cliffs that plunge into the misty valley. Mother, father and child all turn their faces to this celestial watercolour, seemingly unable to look away, so gripped are they by this glimpse, not only of the immensity of the world, but of their infinite insignificance.

They walk another two kilometres, following a path past embankments that have not been mown for many years, past former orchards wreathed in mist that the forests have reclaimed. The split trunks of the hundred-year-old fruit trees overgrown with mistletoe rise up between the bare branches of the beeches and pubescent oaks. Clearly some of the orchards were once ringed by dry-stone walls, since here and there a crumbling outline can be discerned beneath thick ivy and saxifrage.

They also pass the ruins of a hamlet made up of rickety barns whose walls still stand only because they are supported by dense, tufted liana whose adventitious roots have colonized every chink and crack. The roofs have bowed beneath their own weight after the joists and rafters, eaten away by dry rot and woodworm, collapsed, bringing with them showers of slate tiles.

Driving winds and floodwaters have deposited enough alluvium within the heart of these ruins for wild roses and elderflowers to take root, and even hazel and locust trees. Their trunks have cut a path through the rubble. They rise through the yawning roof, spreading their branches above, such that the village barns and the village itself look as though once, in a far-off time, they were inhabited by fantastical creatures who deliberately built these structures so that they would blend into the vegetation.

A red kite in motionless flight hangs over father, mother and son as they walk. Looking up, they can make out the white feathers of its angled wings as, voluptuously, they mould to the currents of warm air. The bird lets out a shrill cry that the mountains return as a single echo.

As they cross a bridge that spans the riverbed, the boy leans over to stare at the water foaming between rocks covered with vivid green moss. Here and there, in pools of still water – water so pellucid that there is no boundary between the tawny, pebble-strewn riverbed and the almost crystalline air of the forest – dappled fish hide in the shifting shadows of the large beds of tape grass.

The mother, who is walking behind, lays a hand on his arm, urging him to move on, and the son adjusts the straps of the rucksack on his shoulders before quickening his pace to rejoin the father.

Before long, they come to a fork from which one steep path winds through the woodland. The father sets his bag at his feet, takes a metal canteen from one of the side pockets, unscrews the cap and brings the canteen to his lips.

With each swallow, his Adam's apple bobs beneath the skin as though about to slice through it. He wipes his mouth, hands the canteen to the mother who takes it and drinks in turn.

'This way,' he says, jerking his chin towards the path.

His breath clouds the air.

'Is it much further?' asks the mother.

'About three kilometres. The going gets more difficult from here on.'

The mother hands the canteen to the child, whose teeth are chattering from the cold.

'Are you going to be alright?' she asks him.

'Of course he'll be alright,' the father answers.

He takes the canteen from the boy's hands, screws on the top and slides it into the side pocket of his kitbag.

'You'll be alright, won't you, huh?'

'Yes,' says the son.

Satisfied, the father nods.

'You see,' he says to the mother.

She gives the boy a half-smile. Once again, they shoulder their backpacks and set off along the path. Day has broken now, but the north-facing undergrowth is still dappled with shadows and the pupils of the walkers' eyes dilate as they move beneath the vaulted gallery of leafless trees, through a grove of beech trees that hides a patch of short grass speckled with violets whose heady perfume mingles with the exhalations of the brushwood. The birds taking cover in the treetops fall silent as they pass.

The son sees groups of marsh tits hopping from tree to tree. Their footsteps startle a jay busy storing its beechnuts in a burrow that has been abandoned by some small mammal. With a rasping screech, the bird takes to the air, offering a glimpse of the metallic blue feathers of its wings. Alerted by the call of the jay, a number of small birds soar from the bushes of blackthorn and dogwood, scattering in a spray of tawny wings only to regroup on the branches of other shrubs, as though drawn by some magnetic force.

The path now winds steeply over the north face of the mountain. Their progress becomes more laboured, slowed by their shoes slipping on the damp soil. They have to be careful where they step on the rocky outcrops and the protruding roots. Their panting breath blanches their lips with each exhalation. The rhythm of progress slows, hindered by the weight of the rucksacks which makes the muscles of their shoulders ache.

When the son stumbles and steadies himself, grabbing onto the father's kitbag, the man stops, turns to him with a harsh glare that warns him to be more vigilant. They flush out an animal with reddish fur that could be a fox or perhaps a stone marten, no-one can say for certain since, in an instant, the animal has silently bounded across their path, disappeared behind a tree, then melted into the shadow of a fallen trunk.

Horizontal threads of pale light pierce the undergrowth, weaving patches of day that strike the bark of the trees. From the layers of decomposing leaves, whorls of steam rise, untroubled by any breeze, and here and there form hazy strata suspended above the ground. As they continue to climb the rutted path, the son fixes his gaze on the father's back, walking in his footsteps and inhaling his heavy breath.

◆

Three weeks before they set off for the mountain, the boy is playing in the back yard when the man suddenly appears. So engrossed is the boy, kicking a half-deflated leather football against the brick wall of the yard that, at first, he does not see him.

The man has come along the alley that runs past the back of the house, stopped at the rusty iron gate. He pats the pockets of his jeans looking for a soft-pack of Marlboro, takes out a cigarette, runs it between his fingers to reshape the finely grooved paper tube as flecks of pale tobacco fall from the tip.

He brings the filter to his lips, tilts his head towards his left shoulder, one hand shielding the flame of the translucent yellow plastic lighter that contains a tiny flickering sea of butane. A light drizzle begins to fall, settling tiny drops on his face, his hair. A dog lets out a bark that ricochets through the jumble of indistinguishable streets and yards in the old working-class district.

He pulls on the cigarette, lips briefly parting over a dense cloud of smoke that he sucks through his teeth and holds in his lungs for a moment. He exhales, a vaporous breath dispelled by the chill wind blowing into the yard from the alley, redolent with smells of soup, exhaust fumes and sticky tarmac.

He smokes as he watches the boy. Sees the nape of the neck where sweat or drizzle has plastered curls of shoulder-length red hair to the skin. Beneath the tracksuit, he can make out the skinny arms and legs, the scrawny body. It would be easy to push open the rusty gate whose creak would be drowned out by the constant thud of ball on brick, to stride across the bare concrete crazed with wide cracks from which tufts of grass sprout from seeds carried on the wind, or dropped from the beak of some bird – easy to wrap an arm around the child's torso, lift him off the ground, perhaps clap a hand over his face to gag him and carry him off. The man could take the back alley and return to the car parked behind the minimarket, which is probably deserted at this hour. He would open the boot, stow the struggling boy whom he could easily overpower, his huge hand gripping a wrist or an ankle before closing the boot.

The man does nothing but stand and smoke as he watches the child kick the ball until he gets tired or bored, or until the downy hairs on the back of his neck prickle, alerting him to the man's presence.

The boy turns and freezes, like a small animal surprised by a swooping raptor. The ball he has just tucked between his elbow and his hip slips from his grasp and falls on the ground, where it lies limply as an empty goatskin.

'Hey,' says the man.

The child glances over his shoulder towards the house, a cramped working-class house built in the fifties, identical in every way to the neighbouring houses that form a block of a dozen grey, dilapidated homes, each with a backyard identical to the one in which the boy was playing a moment earlier.

'Come here a minute, let me look at you.'

The child obeys, but stops at a reasonable distance: should the man suddenly stretch out his arm, his fingertips would not touch him.

The man is tall and thin, dressed in oversized jeans smeared with oil and grease, a red checked shirt over a white cotton T-shirt and an old, threadbare leather jacket. He is still young, though his chestnut beard and hair are flecked with white that glitters when he tilts his head. He has obviously just come from the barber's, because the boy can see a dusting of hair clippings on his throat and the exposed section of his trapezius muscles.

The man asks the boy whether he recognizes him and the boy nods shyly. To indicate his satisfaction, the man nods too. He reaches for the metal gate, pushes it open and steps into the yard.

He is now standing facing the child, and the child looks up to study the face of this man, breathing in his smell of tobacco, damp leather and cheap aftershave.

'You not going to give your father a kiss?'

He stares the boy straight in the eye, then pulls him towards him. He places a hand on the back of the child's neck, presses his face into the fabric of checked shirt, the cotton T-shirt, through which the boy can feel the wiry torso and flat stomach of the father hugging him so hard he cannot breathe.

The father's eyes are misted with tears, and the muscle of his right cheek is twitching. He nods again, as though attempting to fully grasp this moment, to come to grips with this, their motionless bodies embracing in the murky light.

Later, sitting at the kitchen table, his right forearm resting on the oilcloth, the father drums his fingers on the beer bottle he has just taken from the fridge and uncapped with his teeth. He glances around him at the little room that opens onto the small sitting room, the neat countertop, the two chipped white ceramic plates in the metal dish rack.

The son is standing in the doorway. The father nods to the opposite chair, on which he draped his leather jacket. The boy walks over and sits down. The man brings the bottle to his lips, wipes them with the back of his hand. Without taking his eyes off the boy, without so much as blinking, he begins to talk in a low voice, as though this is a mere formality.

He tells the boy to listen to him carefully. He tells the boy that, in his absence, he has probably become the man of the house, that six years without having a father around cannot have been a picnic, but that he is back now and he intends to stay for good, that nothing will ever separate him again from the mother who maybe still loves him, who without a shadow of a doubt still loves him, or who he will win over again if the years she has spent without him have made her distant, and that the boy had better get used to the idea.

He asks the son whether he understands what he has just said. The boy nods and the father leans back in his chair, satisfied. He grabs the pack of Marlboros, shakes out a cigarette and rolls it between the index and middle fingers of his right hand. He taps the filter against the faceted, close-clipped nail of his left thumb, then lights the cigarette and puffs relentlessly. The glowing tip burns the tobacco and paper with the crackle of a brushfire.

'You're very quiet. Cat got your tongue?'

'No,' says the son.

'Good. So, how old are you now?'

'Nine.'

'That's right. Nine. Jesus Christ, the time just flies by.'

The father gives a last pull on the cigarette and drops it into the empty beer bottle. The butt sizzles softly. A wisp of smoke appears from the neck still glistening with the saliva left there by the father's lips and rises above their heads.

'You know, I missed you, little man,' he says in a husky voice he clears by coughing into his fist.

The son says nothing; the father adds:

'I'm fucking starving.'

He gets up, opens the fridge, takes out a plate on which a half-eaten chicken carcass lies in a dark, glossy layer of congealed fat that has encased flecks of herbs and slivers of white meat.

He sets the plate down next to the sink, picks up the carcass, rips away the yellowish skin, thrusts his fingers into the joint between the body and the one remaining leg, runs his fingers along the thigh muscle to the neck of the femur, which he effortlessly separates from the pelvis, then he twists the tibia to separate the drumstick, uncovering the bare white cartilage in the middle of the stump that oozes pinkish juice.

The father leans back against the countertop, brings the drumstick up to his mouth; his curled lips reveal a row of small, crooked teeth stained grey by smoking, one of the incisors is broken. With a lateral movement of his jaw, he removes the muscle fibres. His fingers and the corners of his mouth are slick with grease, juice has trickled over the edge of his left hand, wrist and forearm without him noticing or caring.

He swallows, then sets about gnawing the carcass, shredding the tendons, snapping the soft bones that crack beneath his molars, chewing on one end of the tibia to suck out the marrow, then studying the remains of the drumstick between his greasy fingertips. Finally, he turns back to the countertop and drops the bone on the plate beside the carcass.

He brings his fingers to his mouth one by one, and meticulously sucks them clean. He notices the trickle of juice that runs down his arm and gives it a last lick.

'So, where is she, your mother?' he asks.

'At work,' says the boy.

'What time does she get back?'

The son shrugs.

'Depends.'

'She's gonna get a hell of a surprise.'

And, seeing that the son does not reply:

'I'm shattered. I'm gonna go get some shut-eye in the meantime. Wake me when she gets home.'

He rolls his head from left to right to the muted cracking of vertebrae, brings a fist to his face to stifle a yawn, then leaves the kitchen.

The child listens as the father climbs the stairs, leaning all his weight on every step and hauling on the ancient banister. Staring at the ceiling, he hears him lumber along the narrow landing and go into the mother's bedroom directly above the kitchen. He hears the muffled sound of the man slumping onto the mattress. Then, nothing. The child remains stock-still. His hands are clammy and his heart is hammering beneath his ribs.

A year ago, on the patch of waste ground near the football pitch, on the leafless tendril of a bramble bush, he saw a butterfly struggle to emerge from its chrysalis. Beneath the still shrivelled wings, the mucilaginous thorax was contorted by spasms as the insect attempted to free itself from the fragile casing.

Might his heart not rip through his chest right now, burst into the luminous calm of the kitchen, leaving behind its useless, abandoned body?

Only the hum of the fridge and the distant rumble of the town fill the room, bathed in the glow that filters through the closed curtains hanging from the track above the sink, their cotton yellowing from spatters of grease and the smoke of the cigarettes his mother smokes, ducking under the extractor hood only to stub them out, half-smoked, into a makeshift ashtray – a scallop shell from one of the frozen ready-meals she bakes in the oven – or into the stainless-steel sink.

Were it not for the continuing sweep of the second hand on the face of the wall clock, and the housefly engaged in microcosmic exploration of the oilskin tablecloth, the son would think that the late afternoon light had assumed the density of amber and that time, once and for all, had stood still.

◆

Here, the path is deeper, dug into the hillside; the verge, at shoulder-height for the child, reveals tangled braids of reddish-brown bands of soil, limestone rock, and root systems blindly forging into the space hollowed out by the path.

Mosses and maidenhair ferns, making the most of the barren earth, cling to the steep sides; birds have built their nests here. The son studies the hollows they have carved out among some of the roots, from which they have suspended their fragile structures of twigs, downy feathers and skilfully placed sphagnum mosses, reinforced with the mortar they regurgitate and shape. Now and then something quivers within; soft beaks gape over bright gullets while a faint peeping rises, clamouring for food.

The path rises steeply now, the ground is treacherous; father, mother and son advance in small, slow steps. A spring clearly gushes somewhere further uphill; water trickles to form a rivulet that now runs down the middle of the half-buried path; the rains have carved out labyrinthine clefts exposing flat siliceous rocks on which the soles of their shoes slip and slide.

For support, they lean on staffs made from branches oozing sap ripped from a clump of alders by the father, who has crudely whittled one end with a pocket-knife. They plant the points in the crevices between the rocks. The straps of the backpacks cut into their shoulders, while the sheer weight leaves their backs bruised and their leg muscles cramped. As they continue their ascent, they are forced to take short breaks to catch their breath, shake off their cramps and wipe away the sweat beading on their foreheads and trickling down their necks.

They pass the spring whose presence they intuited some time earlier. It bubbles lazily next to an uprooted tree that, in its fall, ripped from the ground a slab of earth that now stands, dark, menacing and bristling with rootlets above a gaping maw filled by the limpid waters of the spring, towards which the father now bends to fill the canteen. They drink the icy water which catches in their throats and leaves a mineral taste in their mouths.

The father says that the water comes from *up there*, without indicating a direction. The son looks up but can see nothing but the tall conifers with their scaly trunks that blot out the sky. They rest for a moment next to the spring, which overflows the well and streams between their feet.

With the tip of his walking stick, the father points to animal tracks in the wet soil. He fumbles in his pocket for the pack of

Marlboros. Still staring at the paw prints, he inserts the filter between his incisors.

'A fox,' he says. 'Probably came here to drink. I used to have one back in Les Roches with the old man. Tamer than a dog, it was.'

'What was his name?' asks the son.

The father hesitates.

'I don't think he had a name.'

'How long did you have him?'

'Couple of months. A year or two, maybe.'

'What happened to him?'

The father pulls on his cigarette and seems to rack his brain.

'I don't remember,' he says, tossing the cigarette butt.

Then, after another silence:

'Let's press on.'

The mother, who has set down her backpack, almost loses her balance as she tries to shoulder it again. The father grabs her forearm to stop her from falling.

'I'm fine,' she says.

'Let me take it.'

'It's alright, I can carry it.'

For a moment that, to the son, seems strangely protracted, the father continues to grip the wrist until the mother twists her arm and frees herself.

'I'm fine,' she says again in a low voice, darting a quick glance at the child.

The man grabs the handle of the backpack, pulls the right strap over his left shoulder and walks off without a word, with his kitbag on his back and the mother's backpack over his chest.

The mother nods to the son to signal they should follow. While the child once again falls into step behind the father, she lingers by the spring and looks back, trying perhaps to gauge the distance they have come. The path slopes so sharply that it quickly disappears, engulfed by the undergrowth, as though the forest has closed up behind them. Then, once more stabbing the ground with her staff, she hurries to rejoin son and father.

A gap in the forest opens onto stepped grasslands and fluvial terraces created by buttresses of sandstone schist. Here, the air is pure and bracing, though there is no breath of wind, and the grassy areas are covered with a thick fog that slowly flows and spills into the valley. An icy drizzle settles on the faces of the walkers as they follow the narrow track carved out, perhaps by ancient herds, that winds between tall tufts of yellow rye grass. Mother and son study these ghostly heaths that seem to float between earth and sky; the fog obliterates all perspective.

It seems to the boy that they are in the centre of one of those clouds that hug the mountain peaks and languidly stretch out. Then, returning his attention to the father, he sees he is walking with long strides, gradually disappearing, dissolving, abstracted from the reality of the world.

The son markedly slows his pace until all he can make out is an amorphous figure, a shadow in the fog, and he thinks that the father might actually vanish, leaving only the mother and him, the child, to roam this nebulous terrain.

But suddenly, before them, a faint light begins to rise, sharp rays pierce the mist and settle on the grass, creating great pools of light. In an instant, the fog disperses and reveals a sky so white-hot they are forced to turn away, and when at last they look up, it is to contemplate vast green expanses pricked with snowdrops.

To the west the grasslands disappear, giving way to stretches of marl criss-crossed with gullies, where blackened shrubs and clumps of grass have taken root, and, further off, great expanses of forest plunge into the dappled valley. Above the valley, above the foothills and the mountain passes, rise soaring, shimmering peaks. The air is balmy with the scent of cold earth and the tender shoots of wild garlic they trample underfoot.

The father stops and is quickly joined by mother and son.

He says:

'There you go.'

Silently, they contemplate the landscape.

At first the boy does not see the roof of dark slates melted by the sun between the blocks of migmatite and wonders what the father is referring to. As they follow the valley slope, there appears the vast blind wall of an edifice of coursed sandstone built into the mountainside, one of the stark barns or outhouses they glimpsed earlier. They edge down a steep path bordered by banks of nettles. The shoots that ran to seed last year are now papery and chalk-white.

They come to a flat outcrop flagged with slabs of schist of varying sizes and slivers of slate that were probably once part of a roof, since next to the main building there are a number of smaller outhouses, barns or sheepfolds. Of these, all that remains is the ruined shell, a jumble of beams and rough-hewn rafters and lengths of rotting lath. The rubble has provided fertile ground for clumps of ivy and bramble whose tendrils sprout from the carriage doors.

Father and son set down their backpacks.

The man stretches, flexes his shoulder muscles, cracks his neck.

'There you go,' he says again. 'We're here. This is Les Roches.'

A smile reveals the missing glint of an incisor as he stands behind the son, grabs his arms and briefly hugs him to his belly.

Mother and child gaze at the slant wall of pale stone, the doorway with its bowed lintel and the makeshift screen door cobbled from misshapen slats, the two windows with their ancient grey wood frames, each grilled with three metal bars, then up to where the grain loft should be, the gable-end door offset by the listing building, the window with its warped hinges.

The huge black tarpaulin covering part of the gable roof reveals the gradual declivity of slate, the smaller tiles at the roof ridge, the largest covering the overhang. Next to the building is a lean-to, which is further extended by an ancient pigsty now overgrown with nettles.

The mother steps closer to the building, looks at the dilapidated façade, the tarpaulin partly raised by the ridge tiles. Turning around, she considers the view, slowly shaking her head. She runs both hands through her hair then clasps them at the nape of her neck, as she does when the son irritates her or something annoys her.

The father's smile briefly curls into a rictus.

He crouches down and rummages through the side pockets of his kitbag, takes out a metal keyring threaded with huge cast-iron keys and smaller ones of gleaming steel, examining each with impatient gestures intended to hide the trembling in his hands.

Hurriedly, he takes one of the old rusty keys and unlocks the crude screen fashioned from ill-assorted slats which creaks on its hinges, and seems about to crumble to dust, then takes one of the shiny little keys, opens the front door, and plunges into the shadowy building.

The child watches the mother, waiting for a sign from her, but she pays him no heed; she is still gazing at the horizon, the desolate peaks, the bare branches of the treetops framed against the light.

The son follows the father, stepping into the cold darkness of a vast solitary room, with a floor of bare concrete screed, and no furniture beyond a table, two oak benches, a battered sofa and armchair upholstered in dark velvet, a dresser and a fireplace.

In a corner of the room, next to an enamel cooker, and tucked into an alcove, an old feeding trough fitted with a plastic basin serves as a sink. At the far end, on the right, a steep wooden staircase leads to the upper floor.

* * *

The father throws open the shutters and the daylight reveals stone walls bedded and pointed with lime mortar. Two widely spaced metal struts support the main beam.

The place smells of damp sandstone, concrete, ashes and musty fabric.

The father walks over to the staircase, climbs up and opens the gable door. Rays of sunlight burst through gaps in the floorboards and splash the floor below. As the father walks, sawdust falls from the wooden beams, at first in a heavy shower, then as fine particles that form slow eddies in patches of sunlight whose shimmering briefly captivates the son.

The father cautiously climbs down the staircase backwards.

'Watch out. One slip on that thing and you'll smash your skull.'

The son nods.

'Go up, take a look. Your bedroom's at the far end.'

The father is standing in the middle of the room in front of the staircase and the child dares not move; for a moment they stand, facing each other, as though each is waiting for the other to give in. His face streaked by a beam of sunlight, the man heaves a slow sigh of anger or disbelief and walks over to the door.

The son glances over his shoulder and sees the father go outside. He walks over to the staircase, puts one foot on the bottom step, lays both hands on the top step, tilts his head and looks at the upper floor.

The building is hushed, hostile, cold. A shudder runs down the boy's spine as a gust of cold wind blows through the open door and sweeps across the space, trailing dust balls that roll lazily across the concrete.

Hauling himself up, the boy discovers a landing off which three identical bedrooms are divided by partition walls. Timber struts and plasterboard fixings have been screwed into the beams and filled with fibreglass insulation that is still exposed, despite the plasterboard hoist in a corner of the first bedroom.

Bathed in light from the open gable door, a mattress swaddled in plastic and packing tape rests on a bed base with no legs.

An ashtray overflowing with cigarette butts sits on the floorboards next to a battery-powered lamp. The only furniture consists of a dark wood wardrobe and one of those large tin trunks formerly used to transport cargo in the holds of ships and long-haul flights; the dark green paint has flaked to reveal the metal pockmarked with rust.

On top of the trunk is a book about edible and toxic wild plants, a handbook of local fauna, an introduction to astronomy and a mountain survival guide. The books look as though they have been read and re-read countless times; the spines are furrowed with narrow cracks and the pages dog-eared.

The child steps further into the room. Above his head, spun between two beams, quivers a huge cobweb, long since abandoned and thick with dust.

The faint voices of the father and mother reach the boy as a confused murmur. He walks to the gable door and looks at the landscape below, at the slow, solemn, hypnotic swaying of the larches and the tall pines on the edge of the forest.

He sees the mother and father standing facing each other.

The mother stands, left hand gripping her right arm, right hand on her hip in a gesture of utter defiance. While the father is speaking, she is shaking her head as though refusing to listen to what he is saying or dismissing his words, while, for his part, the father is nodding in an attempt to convince her or make her see reason.

The father gestures wildly as he speaks, pointing to the house, the grasslands, the mountain peaks that rise into the impassive sky. When he turns towards him, the son suppresses a shudder. Blood drains from his hands, his fingers prickle with pins and needles; if the father sees him standing in the gable window, he might think he has been watching, spying on them, trying to make sense of the words carried on the wind in fits and snatches.

Heart pounding, the boy considers retreating into the shadows of the bedroom, but forces himself to remain where he is. It is probably too late, his father has probably seen him, and to skulk away now would be irrefutable proof of his transgression, perhaps even of his guilt.

But the father – either because he has not seen the child, or because he does not care about his presence and is not worried about being overheard – turns away and lays his own hand on the mother's arm in a gesture of appeasement, and indeed the mother is no longer vehemently shaking her head, she seems ready to listen to what this man has to say, though she still seems tight-lipped and hostile to his words.

The boy turns around and goes out onto the landing.

Directly opposite are two other rooms. The first, a narrow space beneath the eaves, has been converted into a bathroom. There is an old pink enamel hip-bath against the partition wall. Next to it is a sink with a cracked basin, also in pink enamel, fitted with a stainless-steel tap that is utterly useless since neither bath nor washbasin are connected to a water supply, only to a grey plastic drainpipe that runs along the floor and disappears into a hole drilled into the wall and stuffed with fibreglass. Above the basin, a crude mirror in a white wood frame hangs from a flat-headed screw set into the mortar between two stones.

The other room is a bedroom, as attested by a second plastic-wrapped mattress on a rough and ready bedframe, amidst a jumble of tarpaulins, buckets, tools and sacks of plaster.

The boy sits on the edge of the bed, runs a hand over the cold plastic that covers the mattress. Condensation has collected under the transparent covering, and here and there small patches of mould have laid claim to the fabric. The room smells of damp plaster, stale tobacco smoke and something indistinct given off by the sun-warmed attic roof or the wooden floorboards.

The child looks around the room: he cannot imagine that the father could have spent even a day living within these four walls with his own father. He lies on his back in a luminous rectangle cast by a skylight. He stares through the glass at a dense patch of sky and, as the sunlit attic beams release their heat, enfolding his weary body, plunging him into a hypnotic half-sleep, it seems to him that this same sky is scudding within him.

◆

The child gets out of the chair, stretches the muscles that are numb from sitting still, walks over to the counter and looks at the abandoned plate, at the bones gnawed between the father's pitiless jaws. He opens the door of the cupboard under the sink and the wastebin slides out on its rails. He tilts the plate over the bin, tapping it against the plastic edge until the congealed fat and the remains of the chicken carcass fall away.

He sets the plate down in the sink, then leaves the kitchen and goes into the front hall, where he silently peers upstairs for a moment. Then, he warily climbs the stairs, carefully placing his feet where he knows the treads are secure so that he is not betrayed by their creaking.

The landing is plunged into darkness and the dusty but reassuring smell of rugs and unmade beds, of the doorframes and the copper pipes in the bathroom.

The child moves on tiptoe, running a hand along the wall to steady himself. Beneath his fingertips, he feels the fleecy floral patterns of the wallpaper that is in all the upstairs rooms. In the privacy of his bedroom, when he cannot get to sleep, he likes to dig his fingernails into the flock wallpaper. Lying on his side, he traces little curves, tiny crescent moons known only to him on the infinitely repeated pattern of blossoms and the skilful twining of stems and tendrils.

The mother never got around to replacing this wallpaper, although she planned to do so from the first. The moment she set foot in the house, she vowed to refurbish it from floor to ceiling, since all that was needed was a lick of paint, a little decorating and some new fittings. But she never managed to do anything, for want of time or want of money, or more probably because she hates living in this house with its shabby, almost antiquated décor.

Nor did she ever try to replace the furniture left by the former owners, the frames with their murky reproductions of picturesque engravings that, nudged askew on their hooks from their original position, offer a glimpse of an earlier version of the wallpaper with clearer contrasts and more vivid colours that conjure a bygone era, the house reminding the child that he and his mother are only passing through.

A slanting beam of light from the mother's room extends across the laminate wood floor. Through the half-open door, the boy first sees the foot of the bed, the rumpled blanket that has fallen on the floor and the father's abandoned shoes, scuffed leather clodhoppers that look like work shoes or cheap hiking boots, caked in dried mud that has flaked off onto the beige carpet because the father used the heel of one shoe to prize off the other.

He can also see the father's feet hanging over the end of the mattress, the once-white sports socks black with dirt, the cuffs disappearing beneath denim jeans smeared with oil and grease.

The mirror of the gaping wardrobe that faces the door allows the boy to see the father's body lying on top of the bedspread, red checked shirt balled up on the mattress, hands interlocked over his belly, T-shirt rucked up to reveal a triangle of pale skin, the bony protrusion of the pelvis and the skinny torso that rises and falls to the rhythm of his breathing.

But the wardrobe mirror limits the image of the father by a line that runs from his right elbow to his left clavicle, cutting through the mattress and part of the bedside table on which sits a romance novel whose cover depicts a couple in a passionate embrace next to a raging sea.

The man is holding the woman's shoulders and the woman's head is thrown back as though swooning or fainting or both; he is much taller than she, and dark-complexioned, his face framed by a shock of black curly hair. She is blonde with blue eyes, the palm of her hand pressed against his chest, her parted lips revealing a row of dazzling white teeth.

The image of this couple is endlessly duplicated, with slight variations – the maritime background might be replaced by a sunset or an opulent hotel; the woman might be brunette and the man blond – on the covers of dozens of other books the mother has stored in moving boxes that she has never bothered to unpack, or leaves scattered about the house, shifting from one to the next according to whatever room she finds herself in.

In fact, she would be incapable of distinguishing the characters and plots of these novels; each, with the same infinitesimal variations depicted on their covers, tells of a forlorn woman who encounters a hot-blooded, unmarried businessman with whom she experiences undying passion, such that the mother probably has the impression of reading a single, ever-changing story, a long and comforting read into which she can slip as she does into the warm, foaming baths she takes every night when the son has dozed off, to alleviate the migraines that regularly plague her, and where she too will doze off, a can of beer and a blister pack of painkillers perched on the edge of the bath, next to one of these novels and the ashtray in which a last cigarette burns away like a stick of incense.

The son feels his heart pounding at the base of his throat as he grips the handle of the door and slowly pushes it ajar. He sets one foot on the rug that covers the treacherous old floorboards. He grits his teeth, shifts his weight onto his right leg and steps inside the room.

He contemplates the father's body sprawled in a lozenge of wan light. From the shadow of the frame on the pale carpet, the patch of daylight mounts the skirting board, scales the wall, illuminates a painting in which a woman, half-lying in a grassy field of green and gold, is crawling towards a grey clapboard house.

The young woman's long, dark hair is carelessly tied in a bun at the nape of her neck. She is wearing a light pink dress with short sleeves from whose pleated cuffs emerge two pale, wasted arms with abnormally bony joints. The dress is tied at the waist with what looks like a metal chain, and the young woman is wearing grey leather flat-soled shoes and white stockings.

She drags her folded legs like two dead weights – it seems that she has already dragged herself several metres, since the yellowing grass behind her has been flattened – and, as she rests her weight on her right arm, whose elbow appears to form a knotty protuberance, her left hand seems to be grasping for a fistful of grass to haul herself towards the house on the brow of the hill. But the twisted fingers of both hands curl inward to her palms, like grey talons.

Before her is a vast expanse of meadow ruffled by the breeze, grasses that seem scorched by the summer sun – the sky which lours over hill and house is grey. A flight of birds soars above a barn; some, tiny, are framed against the pale sky, others are crossing the roofline. One of them glides just above the hill, its splayed wings call to mind one of those solitary raptors that hover over tilled fields in search of prey, or a raven about to land in a stubble field.

What the young woman with the pink dress and the flinty hands is straining with every fibre of her being to reach is the house that rises above the hill to the right of the painting; a two-storey colonial farmhouse, seen in three-quarter profile. It looks as though house, landscape, everything, is uninhabited, that the young woman in the pale dress with the grey leather shoes is forever doomed to crawl towards this ghostly house that will endlessly recede as she climbs the gentle slope of the hill, tearing her dress and her tights and grazing the skin of her lifeless limbs while the meadow continues to widen and warp.

The mother happened on this reproduction of *Christina's World* by Andrew Wyeth in a magazine she was leafing through in the waiting room of a doctor's office. The son remembers seeing her glance around the room before slipping the magazine into her handbag with feigned disinterest.

Later, at the kitchen table, she carefully cut out the reproduction of the painting using a ruler and a craft knife, then pasted it to a piece of cardboard and put it into a cheap clip frame she bought in a shop selling home furnishings.

After affixing a length of twine to the back of the frame, she wandered from room to room, a little hammer in one hand and a cigarette dangling from the corner of her mouth, studying every wall, sometimes holding the frame out in front of her as she decided where to hang it. She settled on one of the walls in her bedroom papered with an old floral print that was peeling away from the yellowed plaster.

She hammered in a steel tack and hung the clip frame, carefully straightening it before stepping back to look at the picture. She slipped a finger between her lips and tapped a fingernail against her lower canine tooth.

'It looks good there, doesn't it?' she said, briefly turning to the son who was sitting on the bed.

The child said nothing and the mother continued to gaze at the painting while she puffed on a Peter Stuyvesant Extra Light, her left hand tucked into her right armpit.

'Yes,' she said in a low voice, 'it looks pretty good there.'

She left the room, leaving the son alone staring at the frame that is now bathed in a grey late-afternoon light that highlights the creases in the paper and the fine layer of dust that has settled on the glass. And, as he observes the sleeping father, it occurs to the child that he might have sprung from the reproduction because something – an ominous feeling, an omen – seems to connect the father's return with the indefinable menace that hovers over Christina's world.

◆

When the son opens his eyes again, the mother is sitting next to him on the edge of the bed, with a pair of folded sheets on her lap. The child stretches and looks around the room he does not recognize.

'You dozed off,' she says, before running a hand over the child's forehead.

'Where are we?' asks the son.

'Up at Les Roches, remember?'

The child nods, lays his cheek on his mother's thigh. She brings her hand up to his neck, the child rolls onto his back and the mother's hand slips down to his chest. She can feel the boy's ribcage softly rise and fall beneath her palm, feel his heart beating as, through the skylight, he again contemplates the pale clouds that scud across the rectangle of blue, stretching and dissolving.

'Are we going to stay here long?' he asks.

'A little while, probably.'

'What about school?'

'Don't worry about school. You'll be home before next term starts.'

They fall silent, breathing at the same cadence.

'Can you help me make up the bed?' says the mother.

They set about ripping off the packing tape keeping the plastic cover on the mattress, then take off the cover and toss it in a corner of the room.

They hold a blue cotton bedsheet above the mattress, waving their arms up and down. The sheet billows, setting countless dust particles dancing in the beams that spill through the skylight.

The father appears in the doorway, leans against the frame.

'All good?' he says.

The mother smooths the sheet with the flat of her hand.

'Everything's fine. He had a little sleep.'

The father nods and continues to watch them for a moment.

'Come and give me a hand,' he says to the son. 'We have a lot of things to do before it gets dark.'

He turns his back and disappears down the corridor. The child looks at the mother questioningly.

'Go on,' she says. 'I can finish up here.'

He finds the father waiting outside the building, standing on the projecting ledge of shimmering schist flagstones, smoking a cigarette. The child steps across the threshold, screwing up his eyes, dazzled by the sun pounding the old barn.

'Follow me,' says the father.

He walks as far as the lean-to, also built of sandstone blocks and roofed with slate tiles. The door, made up of timber offcuts cobbled together, is secured by a bolt and a combination padlock.

The father hunches his shoulders, hiding the padlock from the child's view, spins the notched wheels between his fingertips, opens it and pushes open the door in a belch of car oil and grease.

The child follows him into the dark lean-to.

Old furniture has been stored here: a dresser, a wardrobe, chairs with broken wicker seats, a table, all fashioned from the same dark, dusty wood.

The father walks over to a generator which he fires up. The machine lets out a low rumble and a pungent smell of petrol.

'Turn on the light behind you,' says the father, raising his voice and jerking his chin towards something behind the son.

The child turns around, finds a light switch and flicks it on.

A lightbulb shrouded by thick layers of cobwebs casts a yellow glow at the far end of the lean-to, filled with canisters of fuel, opaque plastic containers, a whole arsenal of tinned foods, crates filled with non-perishable goods – the son can see bags of rice and pasta, bottles of cooking oil, cartons of cigarettes – stacked almost to the ceiling.

Wooden shelves line the left-hand wall next to a cement mixer, a jumble of cement bags, shovels, picks, sledgehammers, various tools, basins and buckets, trowels and tarpaulins spattered with plaster.

The father turns to the son.

'With that lot, I don't think we'll want for anything.'

He piles the containers into a wheelbarrow while the son goes over to the china cabinet and opens one of the bottom doors to reveal piles of mismatched crockery, moth-eaten tablecloths or sheets draped over chipped plates. He closes the door, rummages through one of the drawers, in which he finds odd cutlery, some bolts and screws and a few old batteries. But what catches the boy's attention is an object wrapped in a piece of cloth.

He is about to pick it up when the father says:

'You want to know what that is?'

The son raises his pale eyes towards the man looking at him indulgently, without seeming to expect a response. When the child says nothing, the father picks up the package, lays it in the palm of his left hand and uses his right to peel away the layers of grubby cloth to reveal a revolver of dull, smooth steel, the rifled barrel mounted with a bead sight, the grip set with crosshatched plates. Despite the miasma of petrol from the electricity generator, the gun exudes a sweet smell of metal, grease and gunpowder.

'Pick it up,' says the father.

The child warily takes the gun and the father stuffs the piece of cloth in the back pocket of his jeans.

'Look.'

He swivels the son around so that he is facing the door, hunkers down and puts his arm around his shoulders. He cups the child's hands between his calloused palms, raising them to the boy's eyeline.

'You see that little thing there on the barrel? That's called a bead sight. You close your left eye. And this . . .'

He releases the child's left hand so that he can point out the notch next to the hammer.

'. . . this here, that's the groove. You have to line it up with the bead sight. Take your time . . . See how they're lined up now?'

'Yes,' says the son, re-aiming the revolver.

'Now, look past it, as if you were looking down a piece of thread that stretches as far as . . . let's say as far as the little pine tree over there. You see the one I mean?'

'Yes.'

'Hold the grip firmly. Your left hand keeps your right hand steady. You press your right index finger against the outside of the trigger guard. With your thumb, you cock the hammer. That's it. Now, when you've got the sight lined up with the target, you place your finger on the trigger . . .'

The father slips his finger and his son's into the trigger guard.

'Breathe slowly so that you don't move too much, focus on the target, and when you're ready . . .'

He squeezes the son's finger on the trigger. The hammer falls and the gun gives a loud, dull clack that makes the boy flinch.

'Boom,' says the father.

He unscrews the loading gate, pops out the cylinder and they both stare at the empty chambers.

'I've got a few bullets somewhere. We can go fire some real shots, if you want. I'll teach you.'

'Okay,' says the son.

'We'll sort it out later. Right now, we need to go fetch water.'

The father wraps the revolver in the greasy cloth, places it in the cabinet drawer which he slides closed.

He cuts a swathe through the overgrown path. The son follows behind, carrying a long stick he uses to behead the thistles scorched by winter, and before long the father is whistling cheerfully as the wheelbarrow clatters rhythmically and the plastic containers bang against the sides.

They follow the path lined with nettles, then cross a meadow scattered with tufts of comfrey and borage. The scent of roots and milky sap rises from the earth as from a thurible. The sun beats down relentlessly on the backs of their necks and on the heath.

The trees on the edge of the forest towards which they are walking are also transfixed by the sunlight. At this hour, there is not a breath of wind. As they near the treeline, before they even feel it, they can sense the cool shade of the undergrowth carpeted with flowering periwinkles, and the ivy, with its blue-green leaves the colour of sea-foam, that is mounting an attack on the trees.

They weave their way between clumps of pale primroses, fallen ivy-covered twigs that give way beneath their feet. The vaulted canopy of trees carves up the sky, creating patches of light all around. Some of the trees lie on the ground, others, still standing but drained of sap, are grim, grey silhouettes, others have trunks festooned with drooping tinder fungus like huge sea-shells. Still others seem to be waiting for something, their bare branches thrusting towards the heavens. Many of the trees' north-east sides are covered with dense moss and the son stops and lays the palm of his hand against one trunk. A tremor runs down his spine as he breathes in, as though, through his palm, he has absorbed something of this vegetal existence, as though the moss has imparted its essence, which, with the speed of a thunderbolt, has coursed through the complex network of muscles, sinews and nerves of his arm to lodge at the base of his neck, from which it radiates.

They leave the shade of the copse and once again emerge into the dense daylight of a barren landscape where scorched shrubs and twisted conifers have taken root amid the granitic chaos. The ground slopes gently upwards towards ridges formed by batholiths that look bone-white in the blazing sun.

At the foot of a large igneous outcrop that has burst through a fault line in the bedrock, a rill of clear water flows across a bed of gravel, snaking down the sloping ground. The father kneels, hands resting on a flat rock, then bends and drinks directly from the wellspring.

'The finest water in all the world,' he says. 'Taste it.'

The son, in turn, moves forward to drink. The water is so cold he feels a painful twinge at the roots of his teeth.

'So?' says the father as the son gets to his feet.

The child nods.

'There are other springs closer to the house,' says the father, grabbing one of the plastic containers and laying it on the ground with the mouth pressed against the source. 'But there's something I wanted to show you. Come here.'

He walks around the boulder, hunkers down and points to a stone spiral the width of his palm that juts out from the rock.

'What is it?' asks the son.

'A fossilised ammonite. Do you know what that means?'

The boy shakes his head, without taking his eyes off the nautiloid.

'It means that, a long, long time ago, everything you see here was underwater.'

'The water came all the way up here?'

The father extracts his Marlboro soft-pack, shakes out the last cigarette which he brings to his lips before crumpling the pack in his fist.

He explains that, in the beginning, long before humans, long before these mountains existed, there were other, more colossal mountains; that over the course of millions and millions of years, they were worn away to nothing. He also explains that, once these ancient mountains disappeared, the sea covered everything, that everything they can see now was once a raging ocean with unfathomable abysses inhabited by strange creatures, as attested by this ammonite fossil.

The father says that the movement of tectonic plates literally raised the seabed, throwing up new mountains which were eroded in turn by rains and glaciers until they formed the massif on which he and the son were now standing, which, without a shadow of a doubt, had once been higher than they could possibly imagine.

'So, will this mountain disappear someday too?' asks the child.

'Of course. It is eroding even as we speak. But you and I, we can't see it. It would take the lives and the memories of ten thousand, a hundred thousand men laid end to end to see it.'

The child reaches a hand towards the fossil, running his fingertips over its contours.

◆

The man's face looks strangely boyish, turned towards the window, illuminated by the same leaden sunlight that is now slipping down the wall. A steady breath escapes his parted lips.

For a long moment, the spellbound son cannot look away. He knows nothing and remembers almost nothing about the father: he has only a few, faint imageless impressions, fragments of memories. And, stored in a shoebox in a dresser drawer, two photographs the mother has kept.

In the first of these, she and the father are sitting under a sunshade on folding chairs with pale blue backs and white plastic armrests. They are seated at a camping table piled with beer bottles and paper plates bearing the leftovers of rice salad and slices of melon.

The mother is wearing huge butterfly-frame sunglasses and a baggy white T-shirt whose arms are rolled up over her bronzed shoulders. She is also wearing a pair of frayed denim shorts cut from an old pair of jeans that hug her hips, and her hair is tied back in a simple twist held in place by a pen or a small stick. Her elbow is propped on the armrest, her arm raised, her hand half-hides her mouth. Her head is thrown back as she howls with laughter while her bare legs, slightly bent, and crossed at the ankles, rest on the father's lap.

The father is wearing a pair of dark nylon shorts, his bare chest is lean and hairless. He is bent forward in the chair, his stomach forming three folds at the navel. On his upper left bicep there is a blurred tattoo of a snake coiled around a dagger whose blade is angled towards the elbow while the snake's head is slithering upwards over the handle.

His left hand is gripping one of the mother's ankles, and he has his right arm wrapped around her thighs to hold her still. Mouth gaping, lips curled, jaws clenched, he pretends that he is about to sink his teeth into her calf. He is looking at her playfully.

In the second photograph, the father and three other men are posing next to a grey 4x4 parked in the middle of a tilled field on the outskirts of a forest that is invisible but for the dense undergrowth from which some glossy brown tree trunks emerge.

The photograph looks as though it was taken in late autumn or winter: the four men, bathed in the wan light, are dressed in hiking boots and dark canvas trousers with thigh pockets. They are wearing heavy shirts, jumpers, quilted jackets and waterproof coats.

One of the group – the man on the far left of the photograph – is at least half a head taller than the others and wearing a khaki cap, his left arm is raised, his wrist resting on the shoulder of his neighbour, a blond-haired man with pale eyes whose face is half-hidden by an equally blond beard.

The blond man stands with his chest puffed out, a roll-up clenched between his canines, his features contorted and his right eye closed against the smoke blowing back into his face. He has one arm around the back of the man in the khaki cap and the other draped over the shoulder of the father who is the centre of the photograph. Holding the man's wrist against his chest, the father is looking into the lens, chin up, head tilted in a smug or satisfied expression, lips curved into a half-smile.

To the left of the father, the last of the four men sports a crew cut, and wears a red and green checked shirt, with the sleeves rolled up to reveal his tattooed forearms. His right hand is raised, the thumb and forefinger holding a roll-up from which he seems to be taking a deep drag, since he is sucking in his cheeks dark with stubble as he, too, stares into the lens. His left hand is gripping the butt of a rifle that is balanced on his shoulder, the barrel resting against his neck, the tip disappearing behind his skull.

The man to the far left of the photograph is also holding a rifle in his right hand, its barrel also resting on his shoulder, and the father has a shotgun whose gleaming wooden butt rests on the ground while his hand encircles the double barrel of dark metal.

Lying on its side at their feet is the carcass of a stag, its belly turned towards them, its forelegs bent, its hind legs splayed in the stubble field, its powerful neck twisted at an unnatural angle, its head tilted such that the magnificent antlers, with four tines on one beam and five on the other, rise up before the hunters and reveal its left eye. The last rifle – which presumably belongs to the blond man, the only one unarmed – lies across the stag's abdomen.

On the stag's flank, the thick brown coat is marked by a bloody hole that has begun to dry and blacken as the blood spreads towards the chest. Part of the tongue protrudes from the corner of the mouth while its left eye – the only one visible – whose long-lashed eyelids have not closed, seems to gaze with equal dispassion on the jubilant men and the flat expanse of the surrounding scrubland.

The mother has never spoken to him about these photographs and, after the father left, never referred to his existence except by accident, in the course of a conversation, and one she instantly seemed to regret, as though the very mention of his name was like a thin, sharp blade thrust between her ribs. These photos were probably taken before the son was born – mother and father look younger, and the child is absent – but he has often stared at them in secret and cannot dissociate them from his memories.

It feels to him as though he lived these moments, watched the father sink his teeth into the mother's calf, leaving a lopsided bite mark on her skin, as though he felt the sultry summer day beneath the shade of the parasol, shared their joy and their closeness, smelled the cold earth of the stubble field and the stench of the deer's bloodstained coat. He feels as though he remembers the whiff of the smoke exhaled by the men, the smell of their heavy clothes, sodden with rain and sweat.

He has no precise memory of the father leaving. He has nothing but a series of fragmentary impressions of the life they once shared, perhaps invented and partly shaped by the photographs buried in the chest of drawers. In contrast, his mother's physical presence, her ubiquity, so pervades and colours every corner of the tangled web of his memory that he feels suffused, almost pervaded by her.

If he were called on to describe her – which he could never do with mere words – he would probably evoke images of her, jealously guarded memories, moments, snatches of things she has said scattered over time, sensations that are jumbled yet immediate, that would eventually conjure not a portrait, but a distillation, a precipitate that conveyed something of her essence.

Now, at twenty-six, the mother is still young. She gave birth to the son when she was only seventeen, before she had even felt that she might one day wish to be a mother, a fact she once blurted out to the child in a fit of temper, only to knock on the door of the room where she sent him a moment earlier.

She is sitting on the edge of the bed next to him. The daylight streaming through the window illuminates the right-hand side of her face and her neck, still glowing with the red blotch that suddenly appears whenever she gets angry. She hadn't wanted a child, she tells him, had never even thought of having a child, she was only a lost little girl at the time and motherhood befell her like a catastrophe, like a twist of fate. She confesses that she is a quick-tempered and clumsy mother, that she doesn't always know what to do or how to go about it, since no-one has ever taught her.

In the early days after the father left, they shared a small flat with the mother's mother, a grey, long-suffering woman with a face set in a permanent rictus of anguish who sighed at the slightest word or gesture. Life, in its sheer banality, was a constant trial and torment to this woman, whose only interaction with her daughter involved burdening her with an endless stream of advice and reproaches, to such an extent that – for reasons that the child has never known, but has intuited enough never to have felt the need or the curiosity to ask the mother – the two women had a permanent falling out and the younger woman stormed off, one hand dragging her infant son and the other wheeling a suitcase containing all her worldly possessions.

Since then, the child sees the old woman only occasionally, when – whether by accident or by design – she passes by his school and watches him in play in the schoolyard, sometimes summoning him to give him a sweet from the red patent leather handbag she keeps wedged between her arm and her scrawny chest.

She has shortened the shoulder strap as much as possible and wears the bag strangely high, as though it is a precious object coveted by the whole world, whereas – the child knows from having explored the bag – it contains nothing more valuable than a spectacle case, a purse made of the same tattered patent leather, a handkerchief, a contact book, perhaps the gold-plated brooch with the broken pin, and the blue tin box from which she extracts a pine-flavoured lozenge, which the son invariably accepts out of pity or some vague sense of duty, and pops in his mouth only to spit it out as soon as the old woman turns to leave, having first slipped a small, desiccated hand through the railings and stroked the boy's cheek dotted with freckles, her lips trembling as she stares at him with her watery eyes, rimmed with eyelids that are moist and red with unshed tears.

Sitting on the edge of the bed, the mother sobs inconsolably. She begs the child to forgive her, and as soon as he does, blood once again courses through her and the red blotch on her neck fades. She has been relieved of a terrible weight on her conscience. Though her face is still wet with tears, she is laughing now at something silly the son has said, she draws him to her and hugs him hard, kisses the top of his head and his forehead, swears that she loves him more than anything in the world, that he is her son, hers and hers alone.

Ever since the boy was born, the mother has suffered from vicious migraines that force her to take to her bed or to the sofa, sometimes for days at a time.

Unable to bear any light or sound, she seals up the house – if the shutters are closed when the boy comes home from school, he knows a crisis is looming or already in full swing – and asks the son to empty all the ashtrays, since she suddenly finds the smell repulsive, and to put the kitchen wall clock into a cupboard along with her analogue wristwatch, since even the tick of the second hand is unbearable.

He brings her flannels soaked in a mixture of cold water and Synthol, which the mother presses to her forehead and tosses away as soon as they are warm, so that for days the whole house is pervaded by the medicinal scents of menthol and geranium.

With the tips of his little fingers, he massages her temples, where a bulging vein beats out the rhythm of her pulse; this is to regulate the blood flow that is causing the pain.

From an early age, the son learned to shower, dress and cook for himself because, at such times, she cannot do so. She says that the pain is so terrible that she feels like banging her head against the wall, or that she would rather be dead; even speaking is an ordeal for her.

The child learns to live in the shadow of the mother's pain: over time, his movements grow slower and more wary, his games are whispered in the half-light of his bedroom. He is constantly listening for her every movement, her body turning over in bed, her cries, her groans.

When the crisis finally subsides it leaves her exhausted, haggard but tremendously relieved, and she asks the son to come and lie down next to her. She hugs him to her, kneads his arms, his hands, his feet, cups his face in her palms, as though seeking to substantiate his physical existence or trying to mould a small lump of clay, to shape and perfect it.

'My little redhead,' she says, 'my little fox cub.'

As she comes back to life, things seem more real, more vibrant, but more fragile. Sometimes, she will feverishly beg the child to promise he will never leave her, never abandon her, never turn his back on her.

The mother is volatile, uncompromising and passionate, constantly beset by doubts and regrets, by great surges of joy and chasms of despair.

She keeps a pack of tarot cards in the drawer of her bedside table and claims she learned to read the Major Arcana as a girl, or that she possesses a gift that allows her to intuit their secrets, though she has to rely on a little guide tucked into the box of blue, white, yellow and red cardboard to interpret the cards as she lays them out before her, sitting cross-legged on her bed, a Peter Stuyvesant clenched in her teeth, constantly seeking out the promise of money, of work, of better days and, especially, love.

She is happy when she draws The Star, The Sun or Strength, but whenever Death appears from the pack, she quickly recites the description of the card in the little booklet which says that the card does not symbolize physical death, but change, renewal, a better life, a form of rebirth.

Sometimes she hurriedly puts it back on the pile and draws another card. The card that most excites her is The Lovers, although the description in the booklet leaves her sceptical, since it speaks only of selflessness, trust, honesty.

She dreams of meeting a man who will love her the way the father loved her, she says, by which she means with the capricious, cruel love that, to her, is the only possible love, the only one that matters.

But, in the same breath, she will say that she would rather have any other kind of love, any man who would not leave her alone to cope with a kid.

◆

When they get back to Les Roches, the mother is sitting on a pile of slates stacked against the front of the house. From the open door drifts the scent of soft soap, and the cement floor is dark from being sluiced with water.

The son goes over to the mother and holds out a forked chestnut twig.

'Look,' he says.

She takes the branch and twirls it between her fingers. The father pushes the wheelbarrow as far as the lean-to, opens the padlock and sets about unloading the plastic water containers.

'What's this?' she says.

'We're going to make a catapult.'

'Really? And what are you planning to do with a catapult?'

The father emerges from the lean-to, lights a cigarette as he gazes at the landscape, then sits on the ground, a few metres away from them, resting his forearms on his knees and letting his hands dangle.

The burning tip glows against his palm while the smoke that collects in the hollow of his hand quickly trickles through the space between his thumb and forefinger. He watches the child talk to the mother and the mother pretend to take an interest in the piece of wood.

From his pocket, he takes a knife and unfolds the blade.

'Come over here.'

The son walks over to him. The father balances the cigarette in the corner of his mouth.

He takes the chestnut branch and starts to strip away the bark, the ball of his thumb pressed against the spine of the angled blade.

'Now you try it.'

Turning the knife, he passes it by the handle to the child, who sits cross-legged next to him. From time to time, the father leans over to guide the son's hands. The mother closes her eyes and leans her head against the stone wall, letting the sunlight bathe her face. She can hear the voices of father and son as they strip the branch. She inhales the smell of sun-warmed sandstone, soft soap and wild mint.

'Tomorrow,' says the father, as the son get to his feet and brushes flecks of bark from his trousers, 'we'll run a blowtorch over it to toughen the wood.'

Whistling through his teeth, the son mimes tensing a rubber sling, aiming the catapult at various imaginary targets. The father and mother watch as he wanders off into the tall grass.

'He'll be happy here,' says the father, 'you'll see.'

Their eyes meet and the mother gives him a little smile. The late afternoon sunlight has prevailed over her irritation, her doubts. She feels overcome by weariness. The father gets to his feet, walks over and hunkers next to her. He lays a hand on her cheek, allows it to slide across her jaw and takes her chin between his fingers.

'*We'll* be happy.'

She places her hand on his. She looks into his eyes and says:

'I just wish you could get past this rage, this shadow constantly hanging over you.'

The man stares at her, unblinking, seeming to study her face. His eyes make infinitesimal movements, as though trying to register or memorize every detail, every millimetre of skin, before they once again meet the mother's gaze.

'I'll light a fire,' he says. 'The nights up here can get cold.'

After a silence, he adds:

'I think it's time you talked to him.'

The mother nods as he walks towards the lean-to, disappears into the shadows only to re-emerge a moment later with an armful of logs.

Placing a hand on the ground, she pushes herself to her feet, takes a few steps and glances around for the son. Not seeing him, she follows the impression left by the child's footsteps in the grass. She finds him a little further on, lying on his back in the grass, aiming his catapult at a bird swooping high overhead.

'Do you want to come for a walk in the woods?'

She holds out her hand. As he gets to his feet, the smell of boyish sweat and cold earth rises from the bed of matted grass.

Hand in hand, they walk a little way, their bodies closer or further apart according to the rhythm of their steps, and the little obstacles the son avoids by jumping and sidestepping, tugging at the mother's arm.

The setting sun rakes the meadow in a slanting, wintry light that dazzles them. The son lets go of his mother's hand and runs towards the edge of the forest, where the scaly trunks of pine trees, splashed with golden light, exude a resinous aroma. They walk through the dappled shade of the trees, across a layer of red pine needles that crackles underfoot. The son bends down to pick up larch cones which he studies intently and, after careful consideration, stuffs into his pockets or tosses away.

Sometimes the mother overtakes him, stares up through the monochrome branches where new needles have begun to grow, her face mottled with light and shadow; sometimes it is the son who runs on ahead to get to a tree where he swings and pulls himself up onto a low branch.

The mother leans her shoulder against the trunk.

'I have something to tell you.'

From his lofty perch, the son leans down to look at her and the mother turns away and stares into the hushed undergrowth.

'I'm going to have a baby,' she says.

The son is silent, focusing his attention on the gnarled bark as he tries to pull away a section.

'I don't know if it's going to be a little brother or sister yet,' she says.

The son clambers up, straddles a higher branch, leaning his back against the trunk.

'Careful,' says the mother. 'Don't climb too high.'

'Will the baby be born here?'

'No. We'll be back home when the baby comes in the autumn.'

From his vantage point, the son can see the meadow beyond the trees and the barely visible outline of the monolithic barn against the greenery.

He sits motionless in the chill smell of the pines. The mother waits by the foot of the tree, patient, pensive, eager not to rush the child, until he cautiously descends to the lower branch from which he dangles and drops, landing, feet together, next to her.

Cupping the boy's hands in her own, she seems to be about to say something, but gives up. The son slips from her embrace and disappears. She stands alone for a moment in the luminous, perfumed silence of the undergrowth.

* * *

On the night they arrive at Les Roches, they have dinner beneath a bare lightbulb powered by the generator they can hear rumbling behind the thick stone wall.

The fire that the father lit earlier now warms the vast room, and what seemed forbidding some hours before is now alive with the crackle of logs and the flicker of flames. At first, the chimney belched out thick smoke, the pall of which still lingers, thickening the light.

They heat some tins of ravioli, which the mother serves on old mismatched plates. They eat biscottes with pâté de campagne and palm hearts in vinaigrette, and though the meal is frugal, nothing can dampen the mood of the father, whom the wine has made genial and garrulous. He explains his plans for the house, the work he intends to do during their months up at Les Roches: the roof is the first thing he wants to reinforce, before paving the concrete floor, then painting the upstairs walls; all the little projects he claims he has been working on since his own father's death, as time and money allowed.

'And it was no joke, hauling all this shit up here, let me tell you, all the tools and the materials,' he says to his son, leaning back against one of the two pillars behind the table.

He lights a cigarette, takes a deep drag that makes him shiver, blows the smoke out through his nostrils, engrossed in his thoughts.

'But I knew it was worth it,' he says. 'I knew that one day we'd come up here, all of us, together.'

He trails off, then picks up his wine glass.

'To us. To a new start.'

The mother hesitates.

'Aren't you going to toast with us?' she says to the son.

The child nods and all three clink their glasses over the tablecloth. Abruptly, the father gets to his feet and says:

'This calls for a celebration. I'll be right back . . .'

He goes outside, leaving mother and son sitting facing each other.

The mother looks at the child and smiles, reaches across the table and, with her right thumb, rubs away the spatters of tomato sauce at the corner of the child's mouth.

'Look at the state of you,' she said, 'you've got sauce all over yourself.'

The son is wiping his lips with the back of his hand when the father reappears with a small battery-operated radio spattered with plaster or paint and extends the telescopic aerial. The radio crackles as he turns it on and vainly scans the FM dial. Initially, there is nothing but the hiss of static, then he switches it over to AM and manages to tune in to a music station playing Procol Harum's 'A Whiter Shade of Pale'. As he lifts the radio higher, the signal grows stronger, then the father switches off the lone bulb so that the room is lit only by the glow of the fire.

'Go on, get up there,' he says to the son, tapping the table.

'Where?' says the child.

'Onto the table, come on, quick!'

The boy glances at the mother, who shakes her head in helpless resignation. So, taking the hand offered by the father, the son climbs up onto the table and stands among the dirty dishes. The father cranks up the volume and gives the radio to the child.

'Hold it as high as you can and don't move a muscle.'

He takes the mother's hands, she demurs, feebly protests, but eventually gives in and gets to her feet. Enfolded in the father's arms, in the crimson glow of the fire, her head resting on his shoulder, she moves in slow languorous steps as the room is filled with Gary Brooker's crackling voice.

Later, the exhausted son falls asleep on the sofa in front of the hearth. Father and mother sit up for hours, facing each other over cups of cold coffee. The father chain-smokes and the mother takes an occasional drag. On the table, the radio plays a distant Spanish station at low volume. The voices of mother and father reach the son's ears confusedly, along with the smell and the glow of the fire, which the father stokes before throwing on another log.

In his half-sleep, the son senses something calmer, possibly conflated with earlier, perhaps make-believe, memories of a time when father and mother loved each other with a serene, unthreatening love, and even the presence of Les Roches, of the thick load-bearing walls that surround them, the old slate roof above their heads, affords him a nebulous feeling of comfort and happiness.

◆

When the mother gets home from work, she finds the son sitting on the front steps. With a grocery bag in each hand, she pushes open the rusty metal gate with her foot. Seeing the child, she stands motionless for a moment as the gate swings closed behind her, then she crosses the yard.

As she reaches the foot of the steps, she says:

'What's wrong with you?'

'He's here,' says the son.

The mother shakes her head.

'Who's "he"? What are you tal . . .'

She trails off as the son glances at the upstairs window, then she slowly climbs the steps, goes inside and heads for the kitchen. She sets the shopping bags on the table and stands stock-still, her head bowed, without a word. At length, she raises her head and turns to the son who followed her in and is standing right behind her.

'When did he get here?' she asks in a low voice.

'A while ago.'

'What is he doing?'

'Sleeping, I think.'

The mother nods several times, goes over to the son and takes his face in her hands. She pushes away the lock of hair that falls over his forehead, then strokes his temple with her thumb.

'You stay here,' she says. 'Okay?'

Leaving the kitchen, she pauses at the foot of the stairs, wringing her hands. In the dim light of the hall, she looks smaller and more fragile, but there is a stubborn, almost aggressive stiffness to her body, as though she is preparing to come to blows with the father. She mounts the stairs and the son sees her disappear above the line of the landing. He listens as her footsteps move along the corridor to the room where he stood and watched the father sleep.

When she reappears, she walks past the son without so much as a glance. She goes into the living room, picks up the pack of cigarettes lying on a sideboard, lights one and leans against the wall next to the TV. She stands there, smoking, alternately bringing the cigarette to her lips and biting her thumbnail, unable to disguise the trembling of her hands. The whorls of cigarette smoke shroud her in a bluish veil.

She stubs it out, half-smoked, turns to the son and says:

'I'm going to put the shopping away and make a start on dinner. Why don't you go and play outside for a while?'

The sun has set behind the rooftops and the yard is now in shadow. The child picks up the battered leather football and listlessly kicks it against the wall, glancing over his shoulder at the house. Shivering, he finally sits down on the bottom step and strains to catch what is going on inside, but he hears only the indifferent rumble of the town – a car alarm, a child crying, the bark of the German shepherd chained to a breezeblock in one of the yards on the next street – all the sounds that usually make up a familiar, comforting background, but which now seem hostile to him.

The sky is a dark grey wash that hangs over the stagnant orange glow of the town. Fat raindrops start to fall, exploding on the tarmacked pavements, the flagstones of the courtyard, the metal bodywork of the cars. The child brings his legs up to his chest and hugs his knees. When gusts of wind drive the rain against the house, he lets it whip his face and slowly darken the cotton of his tracksuit.

The streetlights in the alley flicker on, spilling the light captured by the downpour onto the pavement. The sky grows darker still and, before long, the chill that has fallen on the town seeps through the rain-soaked tracksuit and penetrates the boy's skin, skin so translucent that now and then the mother will allow her finger to follow the tracery of veins above his collarbone.

He sits motionless for a long time, his face streaming with rain. When, finally, he is caught in the glare of the porch light as the front door opens to reveal the mother, the son is nothing more than a block of frozen flesh, a small rock placed on the top step, and it takes an almost superhuman effort for him to turn and look at her.

She has changed her clothes and is now wearing the faded, shapeless hoodie that makes her look like a teenage girl. It has a single pocket at the front, into which she is constantly stuffing things – her hands, packs of cigarettes, lighters, the myriad objects collected here and there: coins, a till receipt, a Playmobil figurine or an earring.

'I was about to call for you. I thought you'd gone for a wander.'

She comes out onto the top step, pulls the hood over her head and lights a cigarette. She sits down next to the child and puts an arm around his shoulders.

'You're drenched,' she says, hugging him to her. 'You'll catch a chill.'

The son allows his cheek to rest against the cotton hoodie that smells of smoke and the father's aftershave.

'Where's he been?' he says in a half-whisper.

The mother takes a drag on her cigarette, then turns to blow the smoke away from the child's face.

'He's here now,' she says. 'That's all that matters, isn't it?'

'Is he going to live with us?'

'I don't know. How do you feel about the idea?'

The son says nothing and the mother stares out into the street.

A cat with dark fur jumps onto the low wall surrounding the yard and glares at them, resigned to the deluge. For a moment, they sit huddled together in the porch light, watching the rain fall; their single shadow stretching down the steps and across the glistening flagstones.

The mother runs a hand through the son's wet hair and says:

'Run along and get changed.'

The child takes the stairs four at a time and closes the door of his bedroom behind him. The rain intensifies, lashing the windowpane so that the glow of the nearest streetlight flows in liquid waves across the wall.

From the ground floor the son hears the muffled sound of what he guesses to be a game show on the television and the mother's presence in the kitchen, the clatter of dishes, cupboard doors being slammed, water flowing into the sink, and, finally, a laugh.

The boy looks around the tranquil room, the posters on the walls, the play-town carpet on which he has not played for a long time – his model cars are now stored in a toy box under the bed – which has always seemed to him to possess its own logic, its own laws. When he stares at it from his bed, especially at night, the rectangle of carpet is like a window onto a different world, a neighbourhood, a housing estate, perhaps even a little town with its groups of detached houses with yellow walls and red roof tiles – the houses lean backward to reveal sedate façades pierced by tall lattice windows – its dark grey roads with their regular markings, whose intersections and T-junctions repeat to form a perfect geometric arrangement – the carpet, probably bought by the roll, repeats the same pattern twice – the same pedestrian crossings, the same bird's-eye view of trees represented by the same stippled green, but also its shopping centre and fire station.

In the dim glow of the bedroom, from the warm haven of his bed, between the smooth, threadbare sheets, as the child drifts off into sleep, the world of the carpet seems just as real to him as the one in which he lives – this run-down neighbourhood of potholed streets, dingy houses, dustbins spilling their sour breath into desolate yards, the rocky patch of waste ground like a minefield, strewn with rubbish, dog shit and broken bottles – and, by a simple act of will, he can effortlessly project himself into the peaceful streets, the consummate order of the carpet world that is accessible only to him.

In that world, there is nothing to threaten the child. No-one lives there, nothing ever changes, the town appears to have developed and thrived by itself. There, it would be impossible for the father to show up on a whim, or even to exist, just as, in these curiously slanting houses with their homely façades, it would be impossible for the mother to casually prepare a dinner – as though it were an everyday occurrence – at which mother, son and father would sit down on the first night of his return.

The son wakes, stretches his limbs still heavy with sleep, pushes back the sheets and perches on the edge of the bed. He brushes the soles of his feet over the carpet, which, in the dawn light, is nothing more than a pitiful strip of patterned rug. He gets up and walks across the room, sidestepping the plastic soldiers who fell in combat and lie scattered over the battlefield.

The landing is lit only by a sliver of daylight that extends from the half-open bathroom door and traces a pale line over the floral wallpaper, where the vegetation looks darker, slightly wilted. The child goes into the bathroom and, still half-asleep, sits on the toilet, his elbows on his knees, his face buried in his hands.

He sits, dozing, his head slipping from his cupped palms. He jumps to his feet, pulls up his pyjama bottoms. A small halo of urine darkens the fabric of his pyjamas as he flushes the toilet – something his mother is constantly nagging him to do, because she finds nothing more annoying than a dirty toilet bowl – it is the mother who has ordered him to sit down when he pees, so that he doesn't splash the seat or the soft pink mat she set around the base of the toilet – and it is her voice he often hears shouting from the upstairs or downstairs toilets: 'Don't forget to put down the seat!', 'Don't forget to flush,' 'How many times do I have to tell you?', 'I'm not your slave,' or even 'Dear God, what did I do to deserve this?'

As the child steps out of the bathroom, he notices that the mother's bedroom door is closed. She does not usually close it, and the keyhole glimmers with a faint, barely perceptible glow. The son stops dead: he is suddenly reminded of the father's presence, a fact that sleep had wiped away, relegating it to the vague notions that linger on waking, snatches of dreams, ineffable sensations that are suddenly rekindled by some detail – a word, an image, something that cannot be named – and reappear with pinpoint accuracy. The boy creeps over to the bedroom door and crouches down.

As he puts his eye to the keyhole, he sees only a bright glare, then his pupil contracts and he can make out part of the room, the bare back of the mother who is lying on her stomach, her face turned to her left, her eyes closed.

He has to tilt his head to see the father, who is sitting on the edge of the bed, facing the window, his back to the mother, fists resting on his hairy thighs just above the knees. He, too, is naked, his body pale in the dawn light, his back arched, the skin whiter still at the hips where the coarse leg hair abruptly stops.

The father seems to be staring at something through the window, but the son knows there is nothing to see from that place on the bed but the leaden sky over the town. The father glances at the floor, bends down and picks up a pair of underpants, which he slowly pulls up his hips as he gets to his feet and ambles towards the door; the son silently darts back to his own room.

By the time the boy goes into the kitchen, the father is sitting at the table with a cup of coffee. He has put on a T-shirt and a pair of sweatpants. Leaning back against the wall with his feet propped up on another chair, he has already lit his umpteenth cigarette.

'Don't just stand there,' says the mother when she sees the son. 'Come get your breakfast.'

The son sits at the table and the mother places a bowl, a box of cereal and a carton of milk in front of him. She works in a company canteen on the industrial estate on the far side of town and, in the afternoons, she cleans in a nursery school. She is about to head off to work and is wrapping up some biscuits in a piece of foil.

'Try not to forget your lunch this time,' she says, taking an old, crumbling foil package and a blackened banana from the child's schoolbag.

She kisses the son's head.

'What about me?' says the father.

The mother laughs as she buttons up the denim jacket she has just put on, walks around the coffee table, leans down and kisses him on the lips. The father grabs her buttocks and nervously she pulls away, laughing again, shooting the son a look of embarrassment that forces him to turn his head and stare at the list of ingredients on the cereal box.

'See you tonight,' she says.

But she stands motionless by the door, her left thumb hooked into the strap of her old backpack as she rattles her set of keys in her right hand, looking from son to father, from father to son.

She retraces her steps and kisses the top of the child's head before turning and leaving the room. Father and son hear the front door slam and her harried footsteps echoing on the flagstone.

Not daring to look at the father, the son brings the bowl of milk to his lips, drains it, then stands up, walks over to the sink, turns on the tap and rinses the bowl, with his back to this man whose glowering presence he can feel behind him.

He sets the bowl down in the draining rack and is about to leave the room when he is stopped by the father's voice.

'You know what? Why don't you skip school today? Let's you and me spend the day together, just us guys. You go and get dressed.'

That morning, they walk to one of the last barber shops in the town centre, where the father asks the barber to cut the boy's hair; a close crop, shaved at the temples, short around the ears and shaved at the nape.

The barber is an elderly man with a severe moustache and a thick Italian accent. He sits the son next to the washbasin and puts a rough towel around his neck.

The father sits nearby in the murky light from the shop window, leafing through a car magazine.

'How long has it been since this hair last saw a comb, kid?'

The father takes out a pack of cigarettes.

'Is it okay to smoke here?'

'Open the door.'

The father gets up. The bell tinkles as he pushes open the glass door and leans against the frame, lighting his cigarette as he surveys the empty street.

'Come and sit here, kid.'

The barber sits the son in front of a mirror, drapes a black gown over him, tying it around his neck.

'I think I remember you,' he says, glancing at the father's reflection in the mirror.

'Could be.'

The barber nods as he detangles the son's hair.

'Your face looks familiar.'

'I used to come here with my father now and then to get a haircut. But that was years ago.'

'That's right, that's it. That wouldn't be the man they found up in the mountains, by any chance?'

The father takes a deep drag on his cigarette and blows the smoke into the street.

'I thought so,' says the Italian. 'You look just like him. I remember you now. He used to bring you to get your hair cut once a year in spring.'

'Yep.'

'You know, I thought it was you the minute you walked in, but you can never be sure. The little boy with long hair whose father used to tell me to cut it short so you wouldn't get lice.'

The father purposefully turns away and does not answer.

'I'm sorry to ask,' says the Italian, his tone more hesitant, 'but is it true what people around here said about him?'

'What did they say about him?'

'He died of cancer, didn't he?'

'And?'

'They say he spent weeks wandering the mountains like a madman – that he'd lost his marbles, that he died in terrible agony.'

The father sniggers as he blows smoke through his nose. He avoids the son's eyes reflected in the mirror.

'You know, that's one of the reasons why the old man went up to the mountains,' he says. 'He couldn't stand the vicious gossip and the backstabbing.'

'I mean, I don't know, I'm just repeating what I've heard. There was even an article in the local paper, I remember.'

'People would be better off keeping their traps shut.'

'Oh, I agree, I agree. It's hard to stop people gossiping. This is a small town. Besides, everyone here knew your father.'

The father tosses the cigarette butt into the street and spits a gobbet of saliva onto the pavement. The bell chimes again as he closes the door and sits back on the chair. Next to him, a begonia is languishing on a high stool, leaves hopelessly straining towards the window, while the son looks in the mirror at their reddish undersides, the translucent veins.

'Not that he was like that back when I knew him,' says the Italian. 'He was an easy-going man. It was your mother's death, and then that accident he had . . . He never got over it. It must have been a terrible blow. Ending up in that state, with a young child to take care of, it's unimaginable . . .'

For a while, the only sounds to be heard are the click of the scissors the barber runs over the child's temples and the muffled hum of a radio.

'It was his choice to go and live up there,' the father says suddenly. 'He knew it was going to be brutal, but it was what he wanted. The last thing he wanted was to end up in hospital being fed through a tube and having his arse wiped.'

The barber pulls the black gown off the child and snaps it in the air.

'Still, dying alone like that, it's inhuman. I wouldn't wish it on anyone.'

The father says nothing. The barber grabs a hairdryer, which blasts the smell of overheated resistors and burnt hair through the cramped space. Then he holds a small round mirror behind the child's head so he can look at the back of his neck.

'There,' he says, 'the spitting image of your father.'

The father gets up and looks at the son in the mirror, nodding his head in satisfaction.

'How much do I owe you?' he says.

As they step outside, bringing some of the smell of the barber shop with them, a passing van fitted with loudspeakers announces a funfair near the shopping centre in the south of the town.

'Why don't we go take a look?' says the father, overcome with boyish excitement.

The son nods, running his fingers around the neck of his jumper to get rid of the itchy hairs.

They walk as far as the father's car, an electric-blue Citroën BX that sags on its hydraulic suspension. The bonnet and right wing look as though they have been replaced and crudely repainted in a similar colour.

'Sit in the front,' says the father, seeing the child about to open the back door. 'Wait a sec, let me get this out of the way.'

He steps in front of the child and leans across the driver's seat to clear the passenger seat of the heap of empty cigarette packs, beer cans and half-eaten sandwiches wrapped in greasy paper, which he tosses onto the back seat, which is already littered with a duvet, a petrol can, old crisp packets and various unidentifiable bits of packaging.

The car reeks of stale cigarettes, sump oil and aftershave.

'There,' he says, gesturing for the son to sit down. 'It's in a bit of a state right now, I need to give it a good clean.'

They settle themselves in the car, then the father re-opens the driver's door and dumps the contents of the ashtray onto the pavement. As he keys the ignition, the station wagon rises on its suspension, and he flashes the son a smile before pulling out of the parking space.

As they drive to the shopping centre, a steady drizzle starts to fall. All around, the monotone urban landscape flashes past, the crumbling working-class houses whose windows offer a brief glimpse of kitchens or cramped living rooms bathed in murky light; the new housing developments where life is surely as neat and enviable as the world of the play-town carpet, with their shopfronts of pinkish roughcast and bright red roof tiles, the jealously fenced thousand square metres of carefully manicured lawn with, here and there, a swing set standing in the rain or a tarpaulin-covered swimming pool, the harbingers of sunny days.

The father does not speak and seems unworried by the silence of the son, whom he gives a sidelong glance, nodding as though they had come to some unspoken agreement, as though he is enjoying the child's company.

He reaches back and rummages under the passenger seat, grabs a carton of Marlboros, pulls it out and drops it in the son's lap. The car swerves and almost hits the verge.

'Here, pass me a pack,' he says, jerking the steering wheel to right the car.

The son peels the plastic off the carton, the father presses the dashboard cigarette lighter and the element starts to glow as he blindly rips open the pack pressed against his right leg.

'You remember that thing the barber was saying earlier about my old man? About your grandfather?'

The child bites his tongue.

'Well, it's true,' says the father, lighting a cigarette. 'He was very sick. He died alone, up at Les Roches. That's what they call the house up in the mountains, and that's where I grew up. But it was nothing to do with me. I had no choice but to leave when I turned fifteen, for reasons I can't get into right now, but I might tell you some day.'

The son squirms, sinks back into his seat and fiddles with the armrest on the door.

'All I can tell you is that, for years, I hated him. I even wished him dead – and not just once. But when I found out he was actually dead, it was a real kick in the balls. I was devastated, it knocked me for six. They said it was some hiker who found him. He was lying at the foot of a tree, half-naked, curled up like a dead dog.'

He lowers the window, jerkily cranking the handle on his left, makes a vague gesture to vainly wave the smoke out the window.

'He'd been lying at the foot of the tree for days and some animal, a wild boar, a fox, maybe even a wolf, had eaten half his face and his leg. When they brought him down, I had to go identify the body.'

The father slowly shakes his head and stubs his cigarette out in the ashtray.

'Maybe I shouldn't be telling you all this shit. All I'm trying to say is that, over time, I realized that I had my own faults, that I was far from perfect, that it's pretty easy to fuck things up. Oh, don't get me wrong, he was an old bastard, but he had his wounds. And there's nothing worse than a wounded man.'

The father falls silent, taps the steering wheel with the palm of his right hand as he shakes his head and runs his tongue over the edge of his broken incisor. A few raindrops blow in through the open window and settle themselves on the nape of the son's neck.

◆

The father scooped the son up in his arms or hoisted him over his shoulder, perhaps with the mother's help, and carried him up the stairs and put him to bed.

When he wakes in the middle of the night, he has no sense of how he got here and no memory of the previous day. At first, he thinks he has woken up in the little house in the run-down neighbourhood, but even with the shutters closed, some light from the streetlamp should seep through to define the contours of familiar objects: the white chest of drawers, the toy soldiers on the floor. But he can see nothing, not even his hands in front of his face, and his is seized by the fear that he has been struck blind. A long, loud groan rises above the partition walls and the fibreglass loft insulation quivers. The son screams for his mother. He hears bodies stirring in the next room, the rustle of sheets, the father's voice mumbling something unintelligible. The mother appears carrying a torch. The beam sweeps across the room, and the son remembers: the drive out of the town, the trek up the mountain, the walk to Les Roches.

The mother sits on the edge of the bed. She tells him there's nothing to be afraid of, that the groaning is just the sound of the wind in the rafters. She starts to shiver. The fire downstairs must have gone out, and it is so cold upstairs that her words are white clouds.

'Shift over a bit, so I can warm you up a little while you go back to sleep.'

The son lifts the blanket and the mother snuggles next to him. For a long time, they listen to the house as it cracks and creaks like an old raft battered by a storm, to the wind as it carries the cries of the screech owls with their mysterious white faces that nest in the hollow of a dead tree. But, comforted by the warm presence of the mother's body, nothing can reach the child anymore, and mother and son drift off into a peaceful sleep until morning.

The following day, the father keeps his promise, running the flame of a blowtorch over the catapult to harden the wood. He fits a rubber band and a piece of leather to the weapon, then takes a stone from the ground, weighs it in the palm of his hand and arms the sling. The missile soars up into the sky.

'If you learn to aim properly, you can kill birds or even squirrels,' he says. 'I had a catapult when I was your age, I don't know where it got to, otherwise I'd have passed it on to you. I shot animals with it.'

'Did you eat them?'

'Damn right, we ate 'em! Up here, you eat whatever you can find. If you catch anything, bring it back.'

The son nods and slips the handle of the slingshot into the back pocket of his trousers.

'And watch out for bears,' says the father, lighting a cigarette.

'Bears?' says the boy incredulously.

The father sniggers as he blows smoke through his nostrils in short bursts, then turns to the boy. The child is still a little hesitant, but is reassured by the feel of the wooden catapult against his buttock and the rubber sling slapping the back of his thigh with every step. Filled with the pride of men who carry a weapon, he strides off.

* * *

The horizon hangs heavy with mist, the mountain is drenched with the night's dampness. The stones are black and glistening, emerging from the earth like the carapace of some great beast nestled in sleep, as though the mountain itself were a huge slumbering creature and the child is walking across its back.

The russet treetops are lost in the fog and everything seems muted: the caw of the blackbirds in the dark thickets, the monotone glow of the sun behind the mist that hides the sky.

Smells of wet soil, roots and wild chives rise from the meadow as the son tramps on. His mother has him wearing a fleece-lined parka so he doesn't catch a chill, and a pair of boots whose soles make a squishy noise in the grass, tinted blue in the hollows by the dew.

As he reaches the outskirts of the wood, the child pauses for a moment. He turns back towards the now invisible barn. Nothing is stirring, not even a ripple through the tall grasses. In this charged silence, the son feels intensely alone, and is simultaneously aware of his presence in the world, of the nature that unfurls all around, of the vastness and the multiplicity in which his existence was shaped and finds itself in this very moment.

In that instant, he is overwhelmed by his defencelessness: surely a bear might actually be prowling the mountains? If it suddenly appeared and carried him off, the mother and father would not hear his cries; he probably would not even have time to scream. Would someone find his body half-eaten in the woods, like his grandfather's remains?

Even the silence now seems charged with danger. The child takes out the catapult, crouches down and, blindly groping for a rock, scans his surroundings. His hand encounters a stone, he gauges with his fingertips, stands up, arms the slingshot and aims at the shadows and the unmoving thickets, but soon his arm tires and he lowers it: what good would a stone be against a bear anyway?

He warily avoids the outskirts of the forest from which rises the cold, damp, decomposing breath of humus. For a long time, the land rises in an arc across the mountain's flank towards the south-facing slope, followed by a gentle downward slope that becomes more pronounced as he walks on. The mist disperses, light springs from some indefinable source, overlaying everything with a gentle clarity.

Gradually, the pine forest gives way to beech groves and blackthorn bushes which are flecked with white flowers. The grassland comes to an end, and if the child wants to carry on, he will have to move through the silent forest. He first explores the more visible depths, still clutching the catapult. He seems to feel emboldened by his trek, because after a moment's hesitation, he walks into the half-light.

Moving from the open spaces of the grassland to the thick humidity of the forest is like stepping into another universe, as though he has not simply cleaved the clean fresh air of early morning and plunged into the grey-green scents of the undergrowth, but passed through a physical frontier, an invisible permeable membrane. He is reminded of the fairy tales the mother sometimes reads to him, whose tangled forests hide mysteries, dangers and secrets.

He carries on walking, following a chink of light in the vegetation, then stops and listens intently. Beneath the quiet that his footsteps have drowned out, something is rumbling in the deep of the woods, beyond the thin, sparse trees, rising from the dense and knotty heart – a whisper joined by sounds that are unfamiliar to his ear: the hammering of a black woodpecker, the sigh of broken trunks followed by a muffled fall, the yelp of a marten like a burst of laughter.

A shudder runs through the boy and he races out of the forest as fast as he can to escape the shadowy trees following hard on his heels. When he reaches the middle of the meadow, he whirls around and looks back at the forest from whose depths he is being watched by a thousand hidden eyes that, taken together, make up the gaze of the mountain. The child draws back several steps, then turns and runs for the barn.

In the first weeks spent at Les Roches, the father is affable, attentive to mother and son, treating them with great consideration.

He insists that the mother not exert herself too much, though he never mentions the child on the way, so much so that, to the son's eyes, the mother seems haloed by the strange aura that surrounds those whom one believes are afflicted by some mysterious illness or ailment, who are pampered and cosseted, whose every need is anticipated in the hope of meeting their wants even before they know what they are, or to spare them the tedium and the effort of having to express them.

The secrecy that hangs over the mother's pregnancy confers on her a sense of mystery, a new-won dignity. As the days pass, she is overcome by an ill-defined sadness. She does her best to spare the son, smiles whenever he looks her way, affects an unaccustomed joy when the two of them are together.

All these things reach the child through a glass darkly, colouring with a hazy, barely perceptible hue the early days of their new life in the mountains, which he nevertheless experiences as serene and surprisingly carefree, filled with wonder that is endlessly renewed.

Three nights a week, the mother boils water in a pressure cooker on the gas stove, pours it into a bucket to which she adds the same amount of cold water. She stirs the water with a long-handled wooden spoon and dips her fingers in to check the temperature.

Carefully, she climbs the stairs, her body moving ahead of the bucket whose handle she grips with her left hand, using the right hand to steady herself on the steps. The water appears black in the dark plastic pail – a builder's bucket – it sloshes and swells with every step, tracing escalating high-water marks and threatening to spill over.

When she is high enough, she hoists the bucket onto the landing, sometimes helped by the son if he is not already undressing in the bathroom under the eaves. The child waits, standing naked in the shower tray, his teeth chattering, his ashen skin covered with goosebumps, until the mother draws water from the bucket with an old tin cup and pours it over one shoulder, then the other, his neck, his chest and finally his head.

She sits on the floor next to him while he soaps himself, occasionally interrupting his constant babble with instructions: 'Wash behind your ears,' 'Under your arms,' 'Rinse yourself down, you've still got shampoo in your hair.'

The cramped room quickly fills with steam and the sweet smell of soap. When he has completed his ablution, his mother stands up and pours the water left in the bucket over his head. He closes his eyes, pinches his nose, and feels as though he is being enveloped in a warm embrace before the mother wraps him in a rough towel.

After he has finished mounting the plasterboard upstairs, the father sets about repairing the roof. He asks the son to steady the double-section ladder as he extends it and leans it against the façade. The boy watches the father rise above him, the ladder bowing under his weight, then reach the roof line and disappear from view.

Taking a few steps back, he watches as the father walks across the roof to the tarpaulin which has been tossed about and ripped by the wind and now lies pitifully across the slates, bluer than the sky, the blue of a turbid lagoon, its folds and creases caked with soil, pollen and twigs deposited by wind and rain.

The tarp snaps in the wind as the father pulls it towards him and drops it on the ground next to the son in a cloud of dust. Kneeling on the roof, he looks for any cracked or dislodged slates, wriggles them free and sets them in a pile, revealing that the battens to which they were attached have rotted here and there where rain trickled through. The father effortlessly thrusts in his fingers, rips out the rotten sections which he crumbles between his fingers.

'Just look at this shit,' he says.

He replaces the slates and climbs back down while the son leans all his weight on the foot of the ladder. If it were to tip back or fall sidewards, he would be unable to stop it falling. It occurs to him that the father obviously did not ask him to steady it because he thought he might be of help, but simply to give him something to do, to make him feel useful. Staring at the father looming over him, a dark figure framed against the sky, the child suddenly feels small, weak, pathetic.

He steps aside as the father sets his foot on the ground, steps out of the shadow of the barn and stands in the sunlight, staring up at the roof, squinting into the light, eyes half-closed, hands on his hips. Man and boy stand motionless. The father is considering how to repair the roof; the son, who is attempting to read the father's mind, mirrors his perplexed expression.

'It would mean taking down the tiles to see the extent of the damage, and replacing some of the battens,' says the father.

He falls silent and, with a fist, wipes a trickle of sweat from the back of his neck, then adds:

'I don't have the right tools.'

He goes in search of a thick roll of black duct tape, picks up the tarpaulin, climbs the ladder again, spreads the tarp over the damaged section of the roof and tapes up the holes.

The mother appears from the house and stands next to the son so she too can watch what is happening. When the father climbs down again, he stares at them, looking strangely sheepish, as though they had caught him in flagrante.

'It'll hold as long as it needs to,' he says, though neither mother nor son have any idea what this means in terms of time, what conditions it entails, or even the details of their presence here at Les Roches.

Maybe the father means that the tarpaulin will hold until he decides to go and fetch the materials that he needs to repair the roof. Or until late summer, when the time comes for them to head back to the town. Or perhaps until just before the autumn wind and rains, if he should decide to come back up to Les Roches to work on it. They do not know, but the mother, unsettled by the father's sheepish look – or instinctively dreading his response should she query him – asks no questions and merely nods.

The three of them stand, surveying the patched-up roof, until the father lights a cigarette and slopes off, head down, swearing through clenched teeth.

◆

They walk down the lone alley of the half-deserted funfair. Around them, most of the rides are still covered with tarpaulins streaming with rain, the switched-off neon signs revealing their anatomy of dusty bulbs and tubes. A few carnies are busy putting up the side panels of the shooting galleries and the crane crab machines.

The father's mood has once more turned reticent since they got out of the car. He walks side by side with the son, though pays him little heed, and he smokes as he stares at the stalls, speechless and uncomprehending, as though wondering by what logical sequence of events he finds himself, in mid-morning, at a funfair in this dreary provincial town, and what he is supposed to do here.

The carnies peer at the two visitors who have unexpectedly shown up at the funfair at a time when its magic, conjured only by darkness and by artificial lighting, cannot cast its spell, at a time when, contrary to its very nature – a certain sense of enchantment and, perhaps, eternity – the funfair looks utterly banal, a crude assemblage of sheet metal, plastic, signs, garish colours and churro stalls that stink of petrol and rancid cooking oil.

A dark-haired toddler with blue-green eyes, his nose so clogged with snot he has to breathe through his mouth, is perched on the lap of a woman with a mane of white hair who is sitting on the metal steps of a trailer. She is dressed in a long skirt and the child winds the fabric around his fingers and brings it to his mouth to chew, soaking it in spittle. Both stare intently at father and son as they slowly pass, out of step, strangers to one another, each existing and moving through a reality that excludes the other's presence, never exchanging a word or a look, such that it is difficult to believe they are related, which in turn makes them look guilty, of what it is impossible to say, but guilty nonetheless of doing, dissembling or plotting something.

In one of the attractions, covered by a red and yellow tent, a string of drowsy ponies in full harness exudes a smell of sweat, dung and battered leather. The son stops and runs his hand through the mane of a little bay with hollow saltcellars and bony hindquarters. The pony's long-lashed eye offers a convex reflection of the boy bending over him and the slate-grey sky beyond, and the boy can sense the sheer stupor, the abnegation of this animal, its neck bowed, its weight on its left foreleg, in its endlessly recurring wait for the little riders who will appear in the early afternoon.

Hands in his jacket pockets, the father waits until the son tires of stroking the dusty old nag. They carry on through the funfair, moving with mutual indifference. The father walks with a cynical stride, the son more slowly, his gaze lingering on each ride and attraction.

The man sees the bumper cars parked on the black metal track, their vibrant colours, their spangled bodywork glittering in the dim light, the yellow canvas roof and the diamond-plate access ramps. He turns, flashes the son a smile and gestures for him to hurry up.

The boy waits on the sidelines while the father talks to the man connecting cables to a power generator; a hairy paunch bulges between a pair of shabby jeans and a Levi's T-shirt and hangs over his thighs. The son realizes that this is the owner of the bumper car ride when the father nods in his direction. From his pocket, he pulls a few crumpled banknotes, which the carny considers for a moment, nodding at what the father is saying without taking his eyes off the son. He takes the money and, supporting himself on the generator, manages to haul himself to his feet despite the hindrance of his belly, wanders over to a gold-painted tin hut and reappears almost immediately with a fistful of tokens.

The father claps him on the back as though they are now best friends, or have just shaken on a juicy deal, then comes back to the son, triumphant.

'He's going to open up for us!'

The bumper car ride blazes to life, hauled from the depths of its torpor, a shudder jolts through the metal framework, transmuted by the multicoloured lights while the loudspeakers mounted at each corner of the track belt out a disco hit whose bassline sends shockwaves through the son's whole body like an explosion that sets his bones vibrating and his heart pulsing with an off-beat rhythm.

With an easy grace, the father leaps up onto the metal ramp, landing with a clatter on the tread plate; the child follows, mounting several steep steps of the same dull metal. They climb into a bumper car chosen by the son for its dark blue bodywork, the father sits behind the wheel, the son to his right on the black polyurethane foam seat.

The father pops in the first token and the car glides across the metal floor gleaming with strobe lights that streak their faces red, blue and yellow. Before long, the son feels dizzy, the funfair around them melts into a blur of vanishing lines and bursts of hazy colour.

The booming disco continues to beat in his eardrums and quake beneath his skin. He clings tightly to the side of the car; the father's arm is pressed against his and, when he jerks the steering wheel, his body lurches towards the boy. He smells of stale tobacco and old leather, spewing his sour smoker's breath whenever he laughs or shouts. The father's physical presence, the solidity of the body next to him, the reality of his existence, his return, no longer seem so obscure, so menacing.

Something inside the boy crumbles, a hesitancy, a fear, and he surrenders to the car's movements, surreptitiously seeks to make contact with the father, to touch him through the leather jacket in a tentative, clumsy attempt to convey his affection – or what he considers the affection expected of a son for his father, of a child for this man, this stranger who, out of the blue, has been designated his father.

He would like to share some part of the father's joy and so borrows some of the affection usually reserved for the mother and transfers it to the father, already dimly conscious of the difficulty, the awkwardness that governs all shows of affection between men, between fathers and their sons.

And when the man slips an arm behind the headrest and puts it around his shoulder, steering the car now with a single, expert hand, the son feels as though he has managed to win a little of his respect, perhaps even his affection, that the father who, moments earlier, still represented a shadowy, hostile figure is opening himself up to the son, or, by this enveloping gesture, acknowledging him and allowing him a glimpse of the door to that most secret space, his inaccessible, heavily walled heart, but also that he will protect him from now on.

The son feels a burst of pride; suddenly all is right in this world where the nexus and the point of equilibrium is this bumper car, whose dark blue bodywork glitters amid the deserted funfair in the grey morning to the thunderous roar of the loudspeakers.

There could be nothing better in the world, he feels, than to be himself, to be here, under the father's protection.

◆

Spring arrives, sharp as a blade.

One morning, they find the mountain ablaze with shimmering light. The air smells of claggy soil, of clover and grass thick with sap. Rocks glitter beneath a white-hot sun set into a sky of deep blue that it liquefies.

From everywhere comes the song of birds, the chirrup of insects, the cry of unseen animals that lurk in what little shadow remains, in the hollows of roots, under the leaves of evergreens, at the entrance to labyrinthine burrows – patiently dug or bitterly won – hidden by a bent twig.

Sent coursing through the branches of the trees, the sap causes myriad buds to open, their tiny perules silently falling away to reveal the blue-green leaves that unfurl and constellate the boughs with vibrant green.

The forest, hostile and barren only the day before, adorns itself with vaporous whorls, dappled shadows that make it seem less fearsome. Over the grasslands, flowers in their myriad variation open their petals; foraging insects feverishly buzz from bloom to bloom, drunk on nectar. The wind rustles through the branches of the pines, raising clouds of yellow pollen that fill the sky and are dispersed by the breeze.

In the dark chambers of the rotting trunks, pupae prepare their metamorphosis; all around, an army of tiny creatures mobilizes – teeming, crawling, industrious swarms – and begin the mysterious enterprise that occupies them night and day.

As he becomes more familiar with his surroundings, the son ventures further and further. He no longer fears the marauding bear. He no longer feels the piercing eye of the forest trained on him. The mountain appears to have accepted his presence, and now contemplates him with an equable attentiveness.

When he walks through the grasslands, clouds of birds perched on blades of grass eating seeds take to the wing in clouds, startled by his passage. His comings and goings carve pathways through the tall grasses, creating a maze known only to him.

Venturing into the undergrowth, he discovers a half-dead walnut tree with dense roots in which a recess, created by some animal or by natural subsidence, has created a dark hollow. Having studied it at length, he manages to squeeze inside, torn between curiosity and the fear of becoming stuck.

His knees drawn up to his chest, his head resting against the curve of a root, he contemplates the vault that supports the tree, the wall of tawny earth from which glossy stones obtrude. Here in the odour of clay and dead wood he dozes, filled with the sense that the tree protects him, that he and it are one.

In the course of his explorations, he develops a mental map of the area. About half an hour's walk from the house heading towards the valley, he visits the ruins of a sheepfold beneath whose collapsed roof lives a colony of barbastelle bats that take tremulous flight in the red glow of twilight. He also discovers an entrance to an abandoned iron mine overgrown by brambles, and stares, petrified, into the darkness of the shaft which exhales a cold, clammy stench. He throws down a stone, but the mine gives back no echo.

In the evenings, the father tells him the story of the Camacrusa, a bogeyman that prowls by night, carrying off and devouring foolhardy children who linger in the mountains after the sun has set. He describes a monstrous leg, ripped from a corpse in some earlier age, with an eye set into the knee. Maybe that's where it lives, the father says, in the bottomless depths of the old mine, surrounded by the bones of the children it has dragged there.

How does it eat, asks the child, if it's just a leg with one eye?

The father shrugs and says it must have found a way, must have a hidden mouth and teeth that swallows children whole like a snake consumes its prey, and the son shudders in terror, for the possibility that the Camacrusa exists, waiting in the dark depths of the mine for night to fall, seems more believable than the bear the father warned him about. From then on, he carefully avoids the path that leads to the mine and comes home as soon as the sun dips below the dark line of the trees.

Further west, by scaling the ridges that run along the grassy slopes, the child discovers the presence of a herd of sturdy Mérens horses with coats of moiré black.

They shelter under an ancient sycamore whose branches are crusted with lichen: the ground all around is compacted, the bark has been stripped from the trunk. Doubtless there was a time when these horses belonged to humans, but they seem to have returned to a wild state. Their manes are heavy with tangled knots, their hooves are split, and if they were ever shod, they are not now. One of them has lost an eye. From beneath the closed lid with its long lashes trickles a tear that swarms of flies come to feed on.

Among the horses is a dam suckling a pale grey foal that is still unsteady on its feet. When it first sees the child, the one-eyed stallion whinnies and the herd trots off to the far side of the meadow. The boy walks into the golden shadow of the sycamore, into the sweet scent of horses, of the droppings that litter the ground and of plaques of lichen warmed by the sun. He runs a hand over the trunk, the smooth curves where teeth and the horses' constant rubbing have stripped away the bark.

Though excited by the discovery, a vague sense of unease means he does not mention the horses to the father or to the mother. But he often returns, at more or less the same hour and, little by little, the horses grow accustomed to his presence, making only half-hearted attempts to flee, though they keep their distance and watch his every movement.

The foal approaches timorously, ready to bound away. Before long the child can stroke its muzzle, feel its warm, wet breath against the hollow of his hand.

He spends endless hours with the horses, leaning back against the sycamore, currycombing their flanks with a broom head he took from Les Roches, and their coats and detangled manes once again gleam in the waning day, when the sun, swallowed up by the mountain ridge, allows a last beam of light to trickle down the adret.

He gives them names and speaks to them in that universal voice that children use to talk to animals. He tells them about life with the father and the mother at Les Roches, his trips into the mountains, his secret paths and hideaways, the squatting shadow of the Camacrusa, the bear that prowls.

The horses listen obligingly until he grows tired of their silence or has nothing left to say and he wanders off, leaving them to their hidden life, far from the eyes of men, rhythmed by the mountain's days and nights.

The mother sometimes accompanies him on a long walk, following the whims of the child without ever becoming impatient. She accepts detours and pauses during which he studies the spherical web of an Argiope spider with its striated thorax, or plays with a slow-worm, which, curled up in the palm of his hand, looks like a piece of bronze in the sunlight.

Together, they build a den, spend hours in the undergrowth weaving together branches and filling every little crevice with leaves. They lie inside and talk, their eyes following the flecks of light that filter through the leaves to stipple their faces, their hands and their bare arms.

'Are you happy here?' the mother asks point-blank one day when they are lying in the hollow of cool earth that the son has painstakingly swept to mark the boundary of the den.

Having no precise idea of the nature of happiness, he nods and sees a flicker of disappointment flit across the mother's face, as though she secretly hoped for a different answer. Or maybe it was simply a trick of the light, because she says, 'That's good, then,' leans over and plants a kiss on each of his closed eyelids.

* * *

It is with her that he discovers the source of the rumbling deep in the forest, which he had first thought was the voice of the mountain.

Following the dry gravel bed of an old stream lined with shadowy ferns, they come to a hollow where a foaming torrent is bordered by monk's-rhubarb. Huge moss-covered boulders beneath the trees hold back the dark, roiling water as it courses down the slope, now hindered by a rocky outcrop, now bubbling over the river terraces and the pools where it lingers, calm, translucent, teeming with slivers of light and patches of sky.

The son abandons his clothes in the fork of a tree branch and, dressed only in underpants, tiptoes across the rocks, arms outstretched to steady himself, while the mother in turn undresses. She smears him with sun cream and the two of them carefully wade into the water, laughing at the cold that bites their ankles. They hold each other's hands as they wade deeper into the stream, taking care to step on flat mossy stones.

The daylight carved up by the branches of the trees and refracted by the foaming current splatters the mother's pale skin, the distended oval of her belly, her swollen breasts with their large dark areolas. As they move deeper into the water, the son can make out the dark bush, the bulge of her sex through the damp cotton of her underpants.

She has never been prudish in his presence. She considers the child's body a natural extension of her own, is happy to take a bath when he is present, wash her crotch in the bidet, where, in soapy water that quickly turns pink, she often leaves blood-spotted underwear to soak overnight. She pees with the door open then wipes herself with two hastily folded squares of toilet paper without pausing in her chatter to the son, her every gesture performed with the same nonchalance, thereby flouting the unspoken principles learned from her mother that the body must constantly be kept in check, private, shamefully hidden from prying eyes, shorn of all sensuality. The crabbed flesh of her genetrix was always forced into severe skirts that never came above her knee, blouses buttoned at the throat and the wrists, her legs sheathed in opaque tights of sempiternal beige, such that she looks like a bourgeois lady from the provinces whose family fortune was squandered and whose only inheritance was an austere, outmoded or anachronistic wardrobe best suited to a governess or a stern post-war schoolmistress.

Every part of the mother's body defied that of her forebear: her ample curves, her supple skin, the hennaed hair she never styles and leaves to air-dry after a bath, even her smell. Since adolescence, she has worn the same heady perfume, with its notes of vanilla and patchouli that clings to her clothes and her pillow, mingling with the smell of cigarettes.

She dresses indiscriminately, sporting old tracksuit bottoms and baggy jumpers and, in summer, low-cut sleeveless T-shirts, cotton shifts and dresses which she wears without a bra. Most of the time, it seems as though she pays no attention to her appearance, or that she is aware of her natural charm: her sense of joy, her nonchalant capriciousness, the fits of melancholy that can make her suddenly tenebrous, baring the depths of her soul.

Then, just as suddenly, she will be busy putting on eyeshadow, painting her nails, inspecting the clothes in the wardrobe and the drawers. She gazes at her reflection in the full-length bedroom mirror, pinching the curve of her buttocks, her arms, lifting her breasts. She wants to know whether the son thinks she is beautiful, whether he would marry her. She asks him, as she does her tarot cards, whether he thinks she will soon meet someone whom she will love and who will love her in return. And when the child nods his head, busy slipping onto his wrist, his fingers, the bracelets and rings that lie scattered over the lacquered top of a dressing table, she flashes him a simpering smile, takes a few catwalk steps across the shabby bedroom carpet, stops and suddenly falls silent.

She removes the earrings she has just put on, puts the bracelets back in the little jewellery box, falls back on the coverlet and lights a cigarette.

'Oh, look, I don't really care,' she says, blowing the first plume of smoke towards the ceiling. 'You're the man for me.'

Shivering, she lowers herself into the rushing current that comes up to her chest, leaving her breathless. Her reflection quivers on the surface of the water. Their hands and feet grow numb. They climb out and sit on the rocks in a patch of sunlight. They do not say anything. Here, they would have to shout to be heard above the roaring torrent. Above them, the unmoving foliage teeming with feverish birds rises in shades of green.

The mother is lying on her back, one arm behind her head, the other hand on her belly. She turns to the boy who is piling stones to create a dam in a calm section of water.

She watches him as a she-wolf watches her cub, heedless, fearless. The current laps against the barrier created by the son, swells, streams between his legs, taking a different course. A patch of slanting sunlight illumines the gnarled trunks, the shifting strata of the foliage. The air smells of damp stone, warm bark and decaying undergrowth.

Clouds gather above the mountain peaks, a shadow falls across the torrent; the son's lips turn blue. The mother vigorously rubs his arms, his back, to warm him up before they both get dressed. The child struggles to pull on the T-shirt whose neck is too tight and she has to help, tugging on the fabric, leaving his ears red and the mark of the seam on his forehead.

'You're growing up too fast,' she says. 'Couldn't you wait a while? No need to be in such a hurry.'

The water that was beading on the boy's skin now creates dark patches on the cotton T-shirt. They head back. As they walk beneath the blue vault of the pine trees, the mother's face is blank as she once again slides into melancholy. As they leave the forest, the sky above them glowers with coal-black clouds. The meadows radiate warmth.

The son reaches for the mother's hand. He takes the tips of her fingers in his palm, but she does not seem to notice.

The father marks out a south-facing area near the house, about a hundred square metres, which he plans to turn into a vegetable garden. The son watches as he bends down and sprinkles the packets of seeds from the lean-to over the soil: tomatoes, courgettes, cucumbers, peppers, but also tarragon, lovage, oregano; all the things that can thrive at this altitude in poor, acidic soil, he tells the child, and, come summer, provide them with an abundance of fresh food that they can store.

At the first attempt, the cutting edge of his spade hits a buried granite block. He kicks away the divot of earth to reveal an area of grey stone which he stares at for a few long seconds before heading back to the lean-to.

When he returns, he is carrying a pickaxe over his shoulder. He stands on the precise spot where he stood a moment earlier, swings the pick above his head and brings it down with all his might, shattering the stone. He crouches down and picks up a granite shard which he weighs in the palm of his hand before tossing it aside.

He carries on, wielding the pick relentlessly, struggling to turn over the meagre, intractable earth. With every swing, or almost, he has to stoop to rip out a chunk of stone. Furiously, he throws it to one side; a heap begins to form, the rocks slip and slide, slippery with the clay that quickly covers his hands, his forearms and the legs of his trousers.

He pulls off his sweat-soaked T-shirt and ties it around his head, baring his pale torso for the son to see. His tendons, his muscles and his jutting bones move beneath his skin. His back and his sides slick with sweat, he looks like a beast of burden beleaguered by the heat. A thin trail of dark hair sprouts from the waistband of his trousers and extends to the hollow of the navel, the swelling of the umbilicus beneath the skin.

The child is struck by the thought that at one time the father was physically joined to the body of a woman about whom the boy knows nothing, that he nestled in her arms – helpless and harmless – that he suckled at her breast, and nothing then prefigured the sight of this labouring body, bowed by sudden fury at this rocky stretch of mountain.

On the father's left side, the son notices a scar tracing a line some twenty centimetres long across the skin slantwise towards the shoulder blade, as though the father had been stabbed and the blade had struck a bone and deviated its course. The scar tissue looks smooth, like the skin of a newborn baby or a burn victim.

Spellbound, the boy cannot tear his eyes away, and when the father stops to wipe his forehead with the back of his hand and light a cigarette, he sees the child staring at the scar but says nothing.

He seems to have decided to do battle with this plot of land whose obstructiveness is an affront, to remove anything and everything that would thwart his plan, or to give free rein, with every swing of the pickaxe, to a blind fury for reasons the child cannot fathom.

The mother brings him water. The father grabs the bottle and drinks greedily, pours water into his cupped palms to rinse his face. Drops of water catch in his eyelashes and the coarse hairs of his beard. A blood vessel in his left eye has burst, ringing the pupil with a reddish glow, but he does not notice and, his face and chest streaming, he takes up the pickaxe.

Mother and son stand at a distance, she mistrustful and confused, the boy hunkered down, playing with a stick in the dirt, but constantly glancing at the father as he might watch a dangerous animal. The mother tells the child to stay in the shade. Eventually, she heads back to the house, stops and turns back towards them, before disappearing around the corner.

The day wears on, elongating the shadow cast by the pile of stones that grows with each passing hour. The sun burns the father's bare back, his arms, his chest, but when the son picks up a spade and offers to lend a hand, the father curtly waves him away, nodding to the boundary of the plot of land.

Night begins to fall and, beneath a sunset gaping like a wound, he carries on digging, his forehead and his pupils bathed in the crimson glow; later still, as the sky grows dark and the forest lies in the blue twilight, the father runs an extension lead from the lean-to shed and plugs in a work light that casts a stark white beam that eats into the darkness of the planned vegetable garden, and goes back to digging.

Mother and son have dinner alone. She barely touches her food, biting her thumbnail as, with a worried look that wrinkles the space between her eyebrows, she watches the son eat.

After she has put the child to bed, she takes a plate of food out to the father.

'You need to eat something,' she says. 'Why don't you stop and start again tomorrow?'

'No,' he says through gritted teeth.

She looks at the father: his body, haloed by clouds of insects flitting this way and that, looks dishevelled, emaciated in the halogen glare that accentuates the furrows of his ribs, the saltcellars above his collarbones, the sunken eye sockets.

He casts a strangely distended shadow, a vision of disproportionate limbs, an evil doppelgänger that emanates from him, dogging his steps, aping his every gesture, every swing of the axe, every throw of a stone, in a way that is monstrous and terrifying.

The mother shivers in the cool night air, sets the plate on a flat stone and hurries back inside.

She lies awake for a long time, listening to the rumble of the generator from the half-open door of the lean-to. When she finally drifts off, she sinks into troubled sleep, populated by menacing figures.

In the early hours of morning, the father comes into the bedroom.

With one hand on the wall to steady himself, he takes off his clothes then sprawls next to her. He stinks of sweat, of clay, of exhaustion. Lying on her side, she studies his unmoving profile, the early wrinkles on his forehead and around his eyes caked with dirt, the eyeballs moving beneath the closed lids, the rise and fall of his breath as he exhales more and more deeply. Blisters have formed in the hollows of his hands and they ooze pus onto his grubby palms.

She waits until he is asleep before she gets up, gathers the dirty clothes strewn across the floor, stealthily leaves the bedroom.

As she steps out of the house, the black, burgeoning mountain is still sleeping in a dew-soaked dawn pierced by birdsong. The clammy air clings to her skin like a wet tongue. She walks as far as the kitchen garden, her bare ankles wet from the damp grass. She contemplates the ravaged earth, the imposing pile of stones like a sinister cairn. Something welling inside threatens to overwhelm her, the sense of a destiny taking shape in spite of her, one whose course she cannot alter.

Above her, in the sky now growing pale, a peregrine falcon utters a cry that the mountain echoes.

◆

Having used up all their tokens, they leave the bumper cars and head back down the lone path through the funfair, which has been drenched by a fresh downpour that they did not notice in the dizzy whirl of the ride.

The elderly woman with the long white hair and the child with the snotty nose have disappeared. The men have finished setting up the stalls and a few visitors are wandering from one attraction to another out of curiosity or disappointment.

The father buys some churros. Together they sit on the edge of a meagrely planted flower bed. The son holds the greasy cardboard cone containing the steaming churros. The father lights a cigarette, watching as the child gingerly picks up a first churro, which leaves his mouth and chin smeared with sugar.

Out of the blue, he asks: 'How did she manage all the time I was away? She must have had someone who helped out from time to time, no, with the house and stuff? And to keep her company?'

The son shoots a glance at the father before seeming to become engrossed in the cardboard cone, the glistening golden churros, the glittering sugar crystals.

'Come on,' the father says. 'You can tell me. I know your mother. I know her better than anyone. She's not the kind to be on her own for a long time. She's not the kind to wait that long.'

He takes a drag on his cigarette, forms a smoke ring that rises up before their faces and dissipates in the grey air, then exhales the amorphous mass of smoke still contained within his lungs. A little ash falls onto his jeans and, with a vague, unthinking, curiously feminine gesture, he brushes it away with the back of the distal phalanges of his fingers.

'She must have seen other men, no? Tell me who you've seen visiting her.'

The son gathers a little sugar on the tip of his forefinger and puts it in his mouth. He feels the granular, soon-dissolved solidity of the crystals on the tip of his tongue, the taste of the cooking oil that makes his mouth water. He squirms and is about to take another churro from the white cardboard cone when the father interrupts the gesture, laying a hand on the boy's wrist, the long fingers with the protruding knuckles, the cold, dry palm.

'Uncle Tony,' says the son as soon as he feels the touch, in a tone he wishes sounded more offhand, impassive, less eager to please, but which burst from his lips in a single breath, with the terse zeal of a confession.

Although he does not know what answer the father is expecting, nor that he is sharing a secret that could harm the mother, as his tongue touches the roof of his mouth to form Uncle Tony's name, he has a vague yet troubling sense that he has betrayed her.

* * *

Uncle Tony is not the child's uncle. They are not related by blood. Uncle Tony is one of the men in the photograph of the hunting party that the mother secretly keeps in a shoebox, in the perfumed depths of a dresser drawer in the now-empty bedroom on the upper floor of the little house.

Tony is the blond, bearded man with the pale eyes, the puffed-out chest, blinded by the smoke from his cigarette, whose arm is draped around the father's shoulders as the father's left hand grips his wrist, just as it did the son's wrist a moment earlier – though in the photograph the grip is not intended to restrain the man, or to coerce, the father holds it gently, kindly, affectionately – their twined fists resting against his chest over his heart such that, at a glance, it is obvious that there is a particular closeness between them.

For as long as he can remember, the boy has called him Uncle Tony. For as long as he can remember, Uncle Tony has been a part of his and his mother's lives, popping up at times, drifting away at others, though never for as long as the father, never in a way that would make either of them think he had gone forever, always somewhere in the background, someone the son might bump into on a street corner in the town centre, or come home from school to find sitting at the kitchen table with the mother, the room filled with smoke despite the extractor fan running at full power, a toolbox on the chair next to him, the overflowing ashtrays in front of them attesting to the hours they have spent talking – about what, the child does not know – and the looks they give him as he stands in the doorway, schoolbag slung over his shoulder, the mother's gaze as she is abruptly brought back to a reality she briefly managed to escape, waking from a dream, shaking herself, a little ashamed, busying herself clearing the table of the piled up ashtrays and coffee cups, and Tony's gaze, his watery eyes, two limpid pools ringed with dark circles, his angular face invariably pale, consumed by some infinite sadness or some inexpressible regret that has been rekindled by the mere sight of the boy.

Uncle Tony was one of the father's oldest friends, the mother tells him on one of the rare occasions when she confides her memories of him to the son.

They were inseparable, she says, always up for a good time, thick as thieves (closer than arse and underpants, is how she puts it), the blond a man of few words, with the translucent skin – a vein bulging at each temple – quick, fleshy lips half-hidden by the pale blond tangle of his beard, piercing eyes that could plumb the depths of your soul, and the dark-haired man impulsive, hot-headed, always handy with his fists at closing time, always spitting blood.

It was as though the father had come down from the mountain with the sole intention of waging war on the town, and had found in Tony – or thought he had found – an alter ego, a mirror image, or at least a partner in crime for the drinking binges, the village dances that beat like a secret heart in the night, for settling scores in the smudged light of streetlamps or drunken dawns, for reckless drives behind the wheel of a

Peugeot 405 GTI, a Polo G40 (sometimes a stolen Audi Quattro or a Toyota MR2) along steeply winding roads and mountain passes, headlights casting a harsh glare, by turns on the sheer rockface and the vertiginous blocks of darkness.

What he really wanted was to live dangerously, says the mother, there was nothing he liked better than to tempt fate. It was his idea of freedom, his idea of independence; in the end, maybe he wanted to wage war on life itself – the town had only been a backdrop and collateral damage for his revenge – to make up for the time he felt he had lost up in the mountains, under the strict, suffocating authority of his progenitor.

She also says that the father is not the kind of man to let himself be pushed around, better to think twice before crossing swords with him. To her, he seemed uncompromising, blazing with an unquenchable fire. He was always pushing the boundaries. Always getting involved in dubious arrangements that he called 'business', the details of which she never really knew.

Time and again, she told him that he would wind up in trouble, but – out of pride or sheer bravado – he laughed in her face.

She says:

'I took his anger, his violence and his jealousy for passion. I was wrong.'

Although the son hears the mother's voice, although in his mind the mother's voice conjures images of cars hurtling through the darkness, fearless silhouettes, he does not really understand what she is talking about – in truth, she is talking to herself rather than to the child, perhaps to see whether, once spoken, her words might have a particular flavour, might halt the march of time or summon up the ghosts of the past – and the child forgets those occasions when she confided in him, told him stories, details about their youth and their life together, which, had he remembered them, would have allowed him to picture the father, to reinforce the flimsy sketch of his memory, to lay another memory – perhaps another complete fabrication – over the two photographs hidden in the chest of drawers.

Or perhaps the mother's words floated in the space of a room and, having hovered over them for an instant, reached him as he was busy playing play-town carpet or examining the tangled trinkets in the jewellery box. Perhaps they trickled into him, sank to the bottom and settled like sediment, so that while he cannot remember, he can recall them, but only from the depths of a primeval, ineffable memory.

He forgets, and all that remains is the fact that Uncle Tony knew the father, and indeed had a close relationship with him – though, if asked, the son would have been unable to describe the nature of that relationship.

From this former closeness, this mysterious complicity, the son develops a fascination, almost a veneration that wreathes Uncle Tony in glory, as though he had come home from exotic far-flung expeditions, had survived a war or accomplished some great feat.

The black hole in the child's life generated by the father's absence – by the secrets surrounding that absence – confers on

Uncle Tony something of its hold, its power of attraction, its magnetic field such that it seems to the boy that some remanence of the father subsists in him.

Every time he encounters Uncle Tony, the son studies his bearing, his posture, the palpable nervousness in the way he stands in the kitchen or the living room. He never seems to feel quite at home, never knows what to do with his body, taps his foot constantly, stuffs his hands into his pockets and rummages about, twirls a cigarette between his index and middle fingers, and the child wonders which of these gestures he learned from the father.

During Uncle Tony's visits, the mother, too, is alert; not to what she sees of the father in him, but to the way that he disturbs the well-regulated, hallowed, almost liturgical routine that she and the child share, to the minute changes effected by his mere presence – his body, his restive silence, his masculine smell – on the atmosphere of the house, pervaded by homely scents and maternal intentions. The father's absence hangs between them, if not as a distant threat, then as a warning, tracing an invisible line that serves as a barrier, a safeguard, that moves and mediates and inhibits them, and gives their every gesture, their every word a graver meaning.

The father's hand lingers on the son's wrist. When he lets go, the boy, unable to swallow his words, quickly bites into the spangled, golden, greasy dough of the churro.

The father runs his tongue over the chipped corner of his tooth, turns away and stares into the distance as he instinctively brings a fresh cigarette to his lips.

'Uncle Tony,' he says in a low voice, not to the son in an attempt to confirm what he has just heard, but to himself, without a flicker of surprise.

A bitter, disappointing, perhaps anticipated realization, but one that forces him to swallow hard, like a sudden surge of bile at the back of his throat.

◆

Soon, the son comes to feel as though they have always lived at Les Roches. He no longer has any sense of measured time. The passing days merge into a series of impressions, scents, images, lights, sensations all connected to the encircling presence of the mountain.

Violet dawns follow glittering nights of a purity the son has never known, whose stars are set in flawless black. Sometimes, in early summer, he stays out late into the evening, amid the scent of fermented herbs, when the earth exhales the heat amassed throughout the day, through occasional cold breezes, while the darkness is alive with the shrill cries and rustlings of night birds.

He sits far away from the nimbus of soft light that radiates from the house, gazing at the inky vault where fires that existed before the world was world still shine, and feeling the presence of the earth, the vastness beneath him. Dizzily, he thinks of the lives simultaneously played out everywhere across its surface, knowing that somewhere a child is walking barefoot, another is falling asleep in a soft bed, that a dog lies dying in the dust in the shade of a sheet of metal, that a city in some far-flung country is shimmering in the darkness, that innumerable creatures are moving about, animated by this mysterious and insistent force that is life, which courses through each of them.

Puzzlingly, he can also feel the great movement – imperceptible yet vertiginous – that carries everything, including him, through time and space, all lives, human and animal, and with them the rocks, the trees, the blazing stars.

Of these moments, he will retain the memory of an epiphany, of being struck by the true nature of things, which no language, no words can communicate; but what lingers will be little more than the trace of a dream, the sense of something being granted and instantly revoked.

Sooner or later, the mother comes to the threshold and calls him, her swollen figure framed against the glowing rectangle of the doorway. And then everything dissipates and is engulfed by night.

Having cleared the stony patch of land, the father sleeps until early afternoon.

When the son gets up, he finds his mother sitting outside the house. Gazing at the distant line of trees, her fingertips idly tracing circles over the cotton T-shirt that hugs her belly, she does not immediately notice him.

When she turns to look at him, he realizes that she was not present, that it was only her body sitting in the early morning light, that her mind had wandered far beyond the gilded treetops.

She pulls him to her, kisses his warm temple, fragrant as a cat's belly.

'Did you sleep well, my little fox cub?'

The child nods, rubbing his eyes, and allowing her to pull him towards her and sit him on her lap. She wraps her arms around him and twines her fingers with his. Together they gaze at the luminous mountain, the sun captured and refracted by the morning dew, as though something at once paltry yet precious has sought refuge in the grass.

The son feels the mother's breath on his back. She squeezes his fingers and her hand trembles slightly. She tells him about a recurring dream she had in the months after he was born.

In the dream, she tells him, they were in a garden or a park, and she would see him in the distance, the son, older than he was at the time, playing on a swing.

'I couldn't really see your face, but I knew, without a doubt, that it was you.'

Everything seemed happy and peaceful, she tells him, yet she would feel a shadow, an indefinable threat, floating over the park.

She would watch as the frame shuddered strangely, about to shatter, as the son swung higher and higher, and she was struck by the certainty of an imminent tragedy.

She would get up from the bench where she was sitting and start to run towards him. Run in a shambling slow motion, knowing that she would not get to him in time, that the swing would fall apart.

She says that, in that moment, she had two conflicting feelings: a terrible fear at the thought of the child's death, inseparable from her guilt ('I'd think: this is happening because of me. This is all my fault.') and a profound sense of relief at the thought that all her duties and responsibilities towards him would disappear in the moment when the son's life was taken from her.

She also tells him that, deep inside, deep in the fragmented dream consciousness, she thought that, with the death of the son, everything would vanish, that there would be nothing for her to do but lie on the shifting grass and cease to fear anything, since she would no longer have anything to fear; the most terrible thing would have already come to pass.

'I wouldn't even have a duty or a need to be alive for you.'

She rests her chin on his shoulder and he feels her wet cheek against his.

'I'd completely forgotten that dream,' she said, 'but it came back to me this morning.'

When the father emerges, he does not speak to them. He walks over to the patch of ground he has dug, and stands there motionless for a long time, contemplating it, to make sure it was not a dream, that he really did achieve his goal, and then he casually pisses on the pile of stones, and walks back towards the house, whistling – though it is not really a whistle, his tongue pressed against the roof of his mouth allows a trickle of air to pass through, in a shrill and discordant breath – then empties one of the containers of water into a bucket and undresses.

The son watches him as he cups water in his hands, brings it to his face, blowing and snorting as he briskly scrubs himself, tips the water over his head, snorting like an animal again, splashes water onto his dark armpits, his scarlet neck and chest. He slips off his grubby underpants, exposing his hairy genitals to the boy as he roughly washes them.

If the mother's nudity is familiar, incorporeal, the sight of the father's body feels obscene and fascinating; the child cannot look away. The man lathers himself with an old, cracked cake of soap that was lying by the sink. Columns of grey foam stream down his back, his pale buttocks, his hairy legs, and settle on the grass like cuckoo spittle.

The snake and dagger quiver on his arm as the muscles of his biceps roll. The ink fused by time into the epidermis has turned blue, the lines have thickened; it looks like the crude tattoo of a sailor, a convict.

He rinses himself with the last of the water, tipping the bucket over his head, his face turned skyward. The water runs over the scar along his side. He is drying himself with his dirty clothes when he catches the son looking at him.

He pulls his T-shirt over his head and says:

'I promised you I'd teach you to shoot, didn't I? So, go get dressed. Let's go for a wander.'

He leads the boy towards the wellspring, towards the granite slopes, shining in the July sun, all bristling with blades. This time, the father follows closely behind as they roam the light-dazed mountain beneath a white-hot sky.

Initially, they are engrossed in the walk, but in fact the father's silence is filled with words, inhabited by a voice that comes from within and is echoed by the whole vast mountain, or else from without; an ageless, toneless, disembodied voice that dissolves into the ether where it continues to exist.

So, when the father walking behind him finally speaks, the son is not surprised; the voice seems to have preceded itself, to have hung over them for a long time, since before they left the house at Les Roches, or indeed before they left the town for the mountains, so much so that the son could say the words in his stead and, in the moment when the first word forms on the father's lips, the boy realizes that the revolver and the idea of teaching him to shoot were only ever a pretext for the father's words to become incarnate, to unfurl, to reach their one objective, the lone target, the boy's heart.

The father says he has and will only ever have one son, that he is not the father of the child the mother is carrying.

The mother did not deceive him, he says, but rather she betrayed his trust, which is worse, since, in all the time he has been absent, he never imagined her capable of betrayal. And if there is one thing, the father tells the son, in that erratic monotone, one thing a man cannot endure, it is to be betrayed in love.

Doubtless, the son is too young to know what love is, too young even to imagine what it might be, yet the father warns him not to believe anything that people usually say about love, the sentimental twaddle, the empty phrases that probably fill the pages of the trashy women's novels the mother reads with a smug, unwholesome eagerness.

'And which, over time, probably warped her mind.'

So don't, the father says in the same unearthly monologue, don't believe any of it, love is only stimulated by desire, love is just the other name – the acceptable name – we give to desire, in other words to lust, and it will use any means necessary to win the object of its lust.

Love is a disease, a virus that infects the hearts of men, a heart that is already sick, already rotting, already corrupted, eaten away by gangrene since time immemorial, whose depths it would be futile to try to fathom.

'I'm telling you this now for the sake of the man you'll be one day: never fall in love, no good can come of it.'

For humans, more than any other beast that roams this cursed earth, are born with this void inside, this dizzying void they desperately strive to fill throughout their brief, inconsequential, pitiful time in this world, paralyzed as they are by their own transience, their own absurdity, their own vanity, and by the preposterous notion planted in their heads that, in one of their fellow creatures, they might find the wherewithal to fill this void, this emptiness that preceded their existence.

'Just like you might try to fill a grave with a shovelful of earth.'

In doing so, they quickly forget that the void is bottomless, the father says, that this gaping wound in the hearts of men is never sated, never healed.

We love and we experience the illusion of living, we love and we believe we have found a meaning in things, a reason, an order to the chaos, when actually love infects us, corrupts our souls, our hearts. We should love everything equally, or love nothing at all, because to place all one's hopes in a single creature as fallible, as flawed, as devious as a human being, one that contains such abyssal depths, is nothing short of madness.

'It is nothing but an expression of utter desolation.'

And while the father says all these things, he admits that he has not been able to apply these precepts to his own life, having fallen in love with the mother, a love he claims is absolute, incurable and which she nonetheless betrayed by being unfaithful, by choosing to keep another man's child, whose very prospect is already an insult, but whose existence will be a terrible, indelible affront, a snub he will have to see every day, one that will constantly remind him of the mother's betrayal.

And that's why he brought them up here to Les Roches, the father says, his voice now hoarse and barely audible, exhausted by his own breath, his own words, as father and son step into the healing shade of the mossy wood, this is why he brought them up here, far away from the town. To find within himself the strength to forgive, and to offer the mother the possibility of redemption.

But though he has tried his hardest to draw upon his last reserves of compassion, of clemency, the father does not know whether he will be able to forgive her, not simply for having been unfaithful – over time, as their love was reborn from its ashes, the memory might fade or even disappear – but for burdening him with a child whom she will doubtless expect that he look upon as a son; a little bastard who will be the living incarnation of her betrayal, a constant stab wound in the father's pride.

'A constant stab wound.'

They are emerging from the wood when the voice trails away, dissolves, as though vaporized by the light. The son begins to wonder whether the father actually spoke, whether he has even broken the silence since they left the house, but after they have walked a little way through the grass that, wilted by the heat, licks at their bare ankles, the father says he expects the son to support him, as one man to another.

'But also, and most importantly, as a son supports his father.'

He does not ask the boy to turn on the mother, nor does he speak of joining forces against her; they must all work together to preserve the ties that bind them – however much they have been abused, however much they have been worn away by time, by the father's absence, by the mother's fickleness and infidelity – to keep afloat this crew they form, come hell or high water.

No, if the father is confiding these things to him, he says, it is not in the hope of making an ally in a vendetta against the mother, but merely for the sake of justice.

'I think that, at your age, you deserve to be treated like an adult.'

He believes the son is old enough to hear and understand these things that belong to the adult world; a world on whose threshold the child has stood until now, or on whose threshold he has been forced to stand until now by the mother's presence, her influence, her omnipotence.

But from now on, the father intends to treat him as an equal, without fear or favour, something for which the son will be grateful one day, he says, and this is why he is confiding in him now, so that he can appreciate, in all good conscience, what the father has endured, what the father continues to endure

and will endure again, the conflicting feelings he has had to battle, the humiliation inflicted on him, and his great mercy.
'With you by my side, I might be able to forgive her.'

The son nods, not in agreement with what the father is saying, but to silence him, to stop this torrent of mystifying words which he does not really understand, but whose deeper meaning reaches him, branding him like a red-hot iron.

And indeed, the father is quiet now, drained of his own voice, and as they reach the rocky clearing ringed with sickly shrubs near the spring, he retreats into a sullen silence.

His brow slick with sweat, the father crouches down next to the backpack he has been carrying by one strap. He takes out some empty tins and bottles and, while the son watches, he walks some twenty metres and lines them up at the foot of tree trunks scorched by the sun, on flat black rocks encrusted with mica.

The son watches his every move, forced to screw his eyes up by the glittering rocks. The reflected heat is so great that he feels as if he is inhaling his own breath, and when the father turns towards him, he can only fleetingly make out a quavering silhouette framed against the landscape.

The man takes the revolver and the ammunition from the backpack and wordlessly, without looking up, he loads the chamber, exaggerating his movements for the child's benefit, before handing him the weapon.

The son looks at the gun, then at the father.
'Remember what I told you.'

The child grips the gun, whose cold, dead touch and mechanical smell he had forgotten. The father stands next to him, hands on his thighs, his patience respectful, almost reverential, while the son recalls the instructions he received earlier in the glare of a bare bulb, in the rumble of the generator in the lean-to, raises the revolver, and aims at one of the targets lined up by the father.

He lays his forefinger along the trigger guard, then, with his thumb, he cocks the hammer, whose mysterious inexorable workings click in the tremulous air, closes his left eye and squints as he looks down the bead sights.

In the distance, the beer bottle flashes green in the sun, a commonplace object casting a grey-green shadow on the rock; all is still.

He slips his index finger onto the trigger, holds his breath, and fires.

A moment later he sees nothing but the bare, opalescent sky, hears only a constant hissing, then the shadowy figure of the father looms over him.

The recoil from the shot sent him sprawling; his head hit the rocky ground and the gun now lies at his feet. The father extends his hand and the son stares at it, half-stunned, then grabs it. The man jerks him so hard that he is instantly on his feet, shaking as the father unceremoniously dusts him down with the flat of his hand, speaking in a voice that is almost inaudible, or at least indecipherable, drowned out by the hiss. The boy brings his hand to the back of his head, and his fingertips encounter a hard, painless bulge beneath his hair.

The father gets him to lower his chin so that he can check the lump.

'It's nothing,' he says.

The child can hear the voice now, as the hissing dies away, and he thinks he hears the gunshot echo off the rocks.

The father stoops, picks up the gun, and once again places it in his hands, but this time he wraps his arms around the child, as he did a few days earlier in the dusty gloom of the lean-to; he guides the boy's movements, together they raise the gun, together they cock the hammer, together they aim at the unbroken beer bottle still glowing greenly. When the father's index finger squeezes the trigger, the son closes his eyes and the sound of the bottle shattering follows the shot so closely that he neither sees nor hears the target explode, which simply vanishes, disperses in the light.

Through his hands, his forearms, his elbows, he feels the juddering recoil of the now-warm gun, constrained by the father's grip, then the feeling of some tension alleviated by the gunshot. Something has been taken out of him, some small burden that also vaporized with the bang.

'Used to belong to the old man, that gun,' says the father after they shoot three more targets. 'He kept it close to him day and night, "just in case," he used to say, "you never know what might happen," though I never knew what he was talking about, whether it was wild animals eating his face off or hikers venturing too close to Les Roches. What I do know is that the thought of anyone coming near that ruin or trespassing on the land he'd bought from God knows who – for fuck-all, probably – this patch of land, this ruin that no-one but him would have wanted unless they needed to drive a flock of sheep to summer pasture – which is why the barn was built in the first place, for shepherds and even their flocks to live in during the summer months – but the idea that anyone might set foot on this patch of mountain without being invited or authorized by him was unbearable. The first thing he did, even before he even put one stone on top of another to raise these crumbling walls, before he cleared away the first of the many skips of rubble he would have to remove to clear the ground, was to erect a wooden sign, daubed in red paint with the warning: PRIVATE PROPERTY / NO ENTRY / BEWARE, MAN-TRAPS. Though it should have been self-evident to anyone who wound up here by accident – and they could only end up here by accident, while heading for one of the mountain ridges, an unlikely route for an experienced hiker, since no-one would knowingly come to Les Roches to contemplate this pile of fallen rocks overgrown by vegetation – it should have been pretty self-evident that there was nothing here that warranted protection, or privatization, not so much as a gate so they could flout the warning not to enter, much less hidden man-traps. But, even so, he planted his painstakingly fashioned sign, with its shaky lettering traced by his one good hand – the left, though he was right-handed – and from the way he surveyed his heap of rubble and his patch of scrubland it was clear that he intended to reign as lord and master and would tolerate no intruders. In the decade I spent living with him at Les Roches, I never saw him without this revolver tucked into the trouser belt of the overalls that he only ever took off to wash, once in a blue moon when he decided they were filthy enough to swap for another pair – both probably dating back to his years at the sawmill – and even then only for as long as it took for the first pair to spew its muck and grime in a basin of soapy water that quickly turned grey, and dry out in the sun, and so it carried on, swapping one pair of overalls for another while the hems and the waistbands frayed, and the seams gave way, forcing him to spend his nights laboriously darning them with his maimed left hand, laying the trousers across his lap and holding them in place with his right elbow or his forearm. He never wanted me to help, he could never have borne the affront of my even offering to help. I always knew this, so I never offered. Ever since the accident, he had this look about him, the pride or the blind rage of a wild animal that has caught its paw in a trap and would rather gnaw its limb off than allow anyone to come close enough to free it, because it doesn't understand the source of its pain. And even after he had raised Les Roches, after he clawed it from the ground stone by stone, he only ever accepted my help as part of my apprenticeship, but at no time did he expect me to help, not even when he was hauling carts of rubble one by one. He preferred to do the work alone, often by dint of excruciating effort and terrible contortions that, at the time, filled me with pity and shame – and much later with respect – rather than ask a child, even his own son, for help. I realized that his keeping that revolver permanently tucked into his belt was a terrible admission of his weakness, his frailty, that what he most feared was being unable to defend himself and me against all the things he imagined prowled around Les Roches, threatening to appear at any moment and take it from us. In the space of a year, this man, who, before my mother's death and his accident at the sawmill, had been a rash, swaggering, foolhardy guy, had become prematurely old though he wasn't yet fifty, fearful, frightened and humiliated by his own helplessness, by the arm he dragged around like a lump of dead meat, like a log, against which he seemed to wage war each day at dawn. During the years I spent with him at Les Roches, I saw him use the revolver three times. The first time was when the intruder, as improbable as he was dreaded, appeared in the person of a short, skinny man dressed like a sales rep who emerged from the forest carrying a leather briefcase, his patent-leather shoes and the cuffs of his trousers caked with mud, and stepped onto the old man's land, and the old man saw him approaching him with a determined stride as soon as he saw the makeshift camp next to the ruined building. The man introduced himself as an official of the Departmental Office of Public Works and, panting for breath after his long walk, explained that he had been sent by the department office to deliver the letter he was holding, a letter that would have been sent by registered mail if the local postman delivered to this part of mountains – which obviously he didn't – a letter stating that, when converting a building originally intended for agricultural use into a residential property, planning permission must be requested using the form provided by the local council, which form, duly completed, had to be returned so that the cause could be considered by the council and the Departmental Office of Public Works, the sole agencies authorized to issue such a permit. A formality which, according to the land registry the official claimed to have reviewed to ensure that permission had been requested for the plot and for the work already undertaken, the old man had clearly not sought. And all the while the official was droning on in his bureaucratic and censorious voice, my father stood, motionless, his one good hand gripping the handle of his shovel, his crippled arm drawn up against his stomach as though in a sling; nor did he blink when the official complained that he had had to park his car down in the valley and walk all the way up to Les Roches – though he was ill-equipped for such a trek, which had cost him half a day, a pair of new shoes and a pair of trousers that were now only fit for the dry cleaner. Faced with the old man's stony expression, he added that he had neither the age nor the constitution for such a climb – then he looked in stunned surprise from my father's crippled arm to the hand holding the shovel, doubtless unable to believe that the man standing in front of him intended to rebuild this heap of rubble – and furthermore, that all this (he waved vaguely at the mountain, the old man and the rocks) far exceeded his remit as an official at the Departmental Office of Public Works. When he had finished speaking, he thrust the letter he was holding towards my father, as though demanding that he take it, and the old man let go of the shovel, which fell to the ground, snatched the envelope with his left hand, brought it up to his mouth, wedged it between his teeth and, with a jerk of his head, ripped it to shreds before the astonished eyes of the official. He tossed the pieces on the ground, where they fluttered away after briefly catching in the mud-caked cuffs of the man's trousers and invited the official to pick them up and stick 'em where the sun don't shine, adding that he was no fool, that the only reason the official was up here giving him grief was because someone in town had ratted on him, because otherwise the Departmental Office of Public Works wouldn't even know about his renovation work, and the penpusher wouldn't have trekked all the way up to Les Roches to threaten him with his pettifogging letter, this spiteful, shameful and servile notice. He would never yield to the tyranny of a bunch of fascist collaborators who cloaked themselves in supposed respectability and rectitude in order to shamelessly abuse poor and honest folk, he vowed. Nothing, said the old man, nothing sickened him more than the mere presence of this man – whom he alternately referred to as a henchman, a lackey, a subaltern – who should be ashamed of himself for claiming to be simply a stooge in some administrative process, ashamed of kowtowing to some sinister hierarchy like a little Nazi, of coming up here to threaten a disabled man – this was the only time I ever heard him use that word, the only time I ever heard him refer to his disability – to threaten a man on a disability pension, and – worse – to do so in front of his son. A man who had used his own savings to buy a plot of land up in the mountains, who was not disturbing anyone, robbing anyone, or trespassing on anyone's property, who only wanted to rebuild an old barn so that he and his child would have a roof over their heads, so they could have a decent home, something to which every human being should be entitled. To the old man, the presence of the official was an outrage, the incarnation of a corrupt, iniquitous system. He warned the official not to hound a man who had nothing left to lose, who had been driven to the brink of despair when life snatched from him the wife he had loved, the wife he had watched slowly die over the course of two years – two years, can you imagine? – two years of unbearable, excruciating agony, a wife whose death had been so devastating that he was no longer sure that he was still alive, and so he woke every morning, amazed to discover that he was still here, distraught at the prospect of having to face a new day, unsure whether he could do so, even for his son's sake because – to be brutally honest – he no longer believed his child's life was reason enough to get out of bed. Isn't that a terrifying thing to hear a father say, Monsieur le Subalterne – I tell you, it terrified me as I stood, frozen, a few feet away, watching the face of the officer of the Departmental Office of Public Works break down as my old man carried on, tears coursing down the deep furrows that had formed at the corners of his mouth – isn't it terrifying to sink so low that every night as you go to bed you think the best, the most sensible, the most reasonable thing would be to turn on the gas when your son is sleeping? Well, said the old man, now stunned, distraught, desolate, that was the state he was in every morning when he headed off to the sawmill where he'd worked for more than twenty years without the slightest mishap, the sawmill where – if he said so himself – he was one of the most skilled, most experienced, most valued workers, until one day, in the course of a routine delivery, his arm became trapped between the logs, several hundred kilos of seasoned wood that fell off the back of the trailer and, in a split-second, crushed his arm to a pulp from wrist to elbow. And, the old man said to the increasingly embarrassed agent, when he had seen his arm trapped between those logs, he felt an uncontrollable urge to laugh, the like of which he had never felt before, and when his colleagues had rushed to help and lift away the logs, he had been laughing like a drain, a twisted laugh, a laugh that mocked fate, that same fate which, not content with having taken his wife, was now crushing his arm, and he would still have been laughing like a lunatic when the ambulance took him away if the numbness in the arm had not given way to unspeakable agony, to pain like an exploding star whose shockwaves broke over him and over the world, such that he lost consciousness and woke up in a hospital ward forty-eight hours later to find his arm bristling with steel pins, and to be told by a doctor that surgery and physiotherapy would be useless, that the nerves were so damaged that he would never recover his former mobility. Three days later, he had discharged himself from hospital against the doctor's advice and gone home, because he had a kid to look after, and after that day, the day the officer of the Departmental Office of Public Works visited Les Roches, I never again heard the old man mention his arm, not even when the agonizing pain made him groan in his sleep or dragged him from his bed in the middle of the night, forcing him to numb himself with booze and cigarettes and painkillers. And if he was telling him all this, said the old man to the official, who now looked as though he had turned to jelly, it wasn't because he wanted the man to feel sorry for him; he didn't want the man's pity, his pity would have been the greatest insult; no, if he had given him a detailed account of a life of drudgery and misery, it was only so that he, as a civil service lackey and doer of the state's dirty work, might understand that he truly had nothing left to lose, that he would rather go down to the town and put a bullet between the eyes of the cockroaches who had grassed him up – and anyone else who tried to stop him from raising this ruin of a land – than be humiliated, trampled underfoot, stripped of his property and his rights. There are things that no man can endure if he wants to remain a man, and it's up to the individual to decide the limits of his honour, what is and is not acceptable to him; in short, where the boundary of his dignity lies. This is what the old man said before lifting his shirt tail to reveal the revolver tucked into the belt of his trousers, its butt resting against his grubby, hairy belly, and the little official, now drained of blood, assured him that a solution could be found, that these things were merely a formality, and that, moreover, his authority as a representative of the Office of Public Works included the power to close the file, something he would promptly do if the old man was prepared to assure him that the barn would be restored to its former state, though he didn't give the old man time to make any such assurance, since he turned and fled, galloping across the meadow, clutching his leather briefcase, glancing over his shoulder occasionally to make sure he wasn't in the line of fire before he finally disappeared into the shadows of the trees, never to be heard from again. But my old man never forgot the official's visit; he brooded about it for years, muttering threats into his shaggy beard against the town council, and – worse – against those who had grassed him up. Rather than fading and disappearing with time, the incident – the memory of this incident – seemed to grow, as though in some parallel universe it continued to recur, and the old man constantly relived the scene, studying it from every angle, imagining new details, repeating the same lines, coming up with other, slicker comebacks he could have said, grumbling about those plotting against him in the town, endlessly adding to the list of anonymous conspirators, of traitors who had cheerfully sold him out, probably because he was on a disability pension and no longer had to work, or maybe because he'd battered a few people – though in a fair fight – back when he was hale and hearty, or maybe because he'd finally turned his back on the lot of them one night when he was in his cups, telling them in no uncertain terms that they were a shower of shits, saying one or the other was to blame for the sawmill accident that had cost him the use of an arm. Maybe it's stupid to say that, after the official's visit, he was never the same again, given that he was never the same whatever the reason – he was never the same after my mother's death, he was never the same after the accident – but still, if there are events that mark a man's life with a red-hot iron, this was one of them. From that day, his one goal was to finish building Les Roches, and his one obsessive fear was that something or someone from the outside world would suddenly appear and try to stop him. What was stopping him was nothing external, nothing from the town, where people had forgotten him, or at least had tired of retelling the story of the sawmill and what had ensued, and before long they ceased to talk about it at all, at least until I came back, until I rekindled the suppressed memory of the old devil – which was what my father was for many of them – an old devil relegated to some dark corner of their minds, with other shadowy things, and then they assumed that I had come to avenge him, perhaps even that he had sent me back with the sole aim of clearing his name after having fashioned me, in my years up in the mountains with him, into the instrument, the right arm of his vengeance; in this, they were partly mistaken. No, the only thing stopping him from realizing his project, from completing the restoration of Les Roches and keeping me by his side, was what he had become: a madman plagued with remorse because he had been unable to save the woman he loved, because he had survived her, a madman consumed with anger and bitterness, constantly reliving the day of the accident so he could point the finger of blame, finally coming to believe that it had not been an accident, but a deliberate action perpetrated against him with the intention of damaging or even destroying him – much later, I learned from a guy who was at the sawmill that day, a guy I have every reason to believe, that it was the old man himself who, distraught at my mother's death and exhausted from too many sleepless nights and too much bad wine, had forgotten one of the basic safety rules and triggered the collapse of the logs that cost him the use of his arm – a madman destroyed by pride, by arrogance and, ultimately, a madman sapped by the excruciating pain that never ceased to rack him – on a night before heavy rains, for example – and would send him running from the tent, and later from the house when we managed to put a roof on it, send him tearing into the mountains, into the black heart of the forest, where he could howl and prowl like a wounded animal, like a demon from some terrifying tale or ancient legend of the kind he would often tell around the fire to frighten me and discourage me from leaving Les Roches. On those nights, as I lay on a pile of blankets under canvas, or later on a mattress that the old man brought back from the dump, I would hear him get up, hear him banging his head against the walls and muttering before he left the house, and I knew that it was not really my father moving about, but something else, something that neither I nor anyone else wanted to face. But one night, I plucked up my courage and got out of bed just after he had left. I saw him stumble towards the forest beneath the pale moonlight that gave everything a strange, blue, dreamlike glow, and he was holding an axe handle in his good hand. I went back to bed, where I tossed and turned all night until I heard him come back in the morning, and when I woke a few hours later, I was no longer sure whether I'd seen him walk away carrying the axe or whether I'd dreamt it, but I remembered the direction I thought I'd seen him take, so, making the most of the fact that he had slipped into a comatose sleep, I took the same path. It was easy to follow the footsteps he had left in the grass as far as the edge of the forest, and from there I kept walking, with no idea what I was looking for. But after half an hour, I realized what he did in the heart of the forest, armed with an axe, on nights when the pain became unbearable. There, on a slope, was a grove of birch trees – I never knew why he chose birch trees, perhaps it was random, perhaps because their pale bark made them more visible in the half-light, perhaps because he found their spectral beauty unendurable, perhaps because he saw his pain as white, white and luminous, like a birch tree in the night – so, anyway, this hillside was bristling with birch trees whose trunks bore the wounds left by his axe, there was no logic to it, he was not trying to cut them down, it was as though he wanted to *slaughter* them; it was a hideous, shocking sight, seeing those trees oozing sap from every wound, sap that seemed to be vainly trying to fill those wounds, flowing down the trunks in a silent cascade of tears. I couldn't help but imagine him, relentlessly swinging his axe with the clumsy grotesqueness of his crippled arm, roaring, lashing out in all directions, moving from tree to tree in a sort of demonic, sacrilegious trance, like a disjointed puppet, and all to staunch the pain and rage eating away at him, and so I ran away, vowing never, never to set foot in that part of the forest again. But I have never forgotten those birch trees, they've come to me in dreams every night since, pale ghosts pierced by stigmata, bathed in resinous tears. It was only much later that I realized that if they continued to appear to me in dreams, it was because, despite myself, in my years in the mountains something of the old man had seeped into me, his pain, his madness had insidiously, surreptitiously infected me. That's where the people in the town were partly but not completely wrong in believing that the old man had fashioned me into the right arm of his vengeance, because when I resolved to turn my back on him, long after I discovered the mutilated birch trees, when I decided to leave Les Roches, never to come back while he was still alive, I had no thought of avenging him, but already, without knowing it, I was carrying inside me the deep-rooted seed of his hatred and his bitterness. The second time I saw him pull the gun was when I decided I had had enough, enough of this backbreaking work, never-ending work, enough of the isolation, enough of his tyranny. I told him that I was leaving because I was seventeen, because I was not afraid of him anymore, because he was no longer the fearsome figure he had seemed to me (and which, by then, he probably hadn't been for a long time), but a pathetic old codger, with his long white hair and the tow-coloured beard that he never trimmed, nothing but skin stretched over bone. Les Roches had finally sucked the marrow from him, it had beaten him. I stood ramrod-straight in front of him, without even a bundle slung over my shoulder, and told him that I was leaving and he would never see me again. His lips twitched, he grabbed the butt of the gun, pressed the barrel to his temple and, in a strange, toneless voice, said that if I left, he'd kill himself, that he'd have no choice but to kill himself, and that even if it was his hand that held the gun, the blood would be on my hands, that sole responsibility for his death would fall on me, the deserter, the parricide. I realized then that what he'd been so afraid of all this time, more than physical pain, more than an invasion by the barbarian horde, was that his son would be taken from him just as his wife had been taken from him; that what most terrified him was solitude, being left alone, without an ally, with only his demons for company. He looked so abject, his bloodless lips quivering beneath his white beard, that I turned away so that this devastating image would not be my lasting memory of him. I headed down to the town, I walked and walked and walked, expecting at any moment to hear a gunshot and the thud of a body on the cursed earth of Les Roches, and hours later, after I reached the town, I still thought that I might hear the echo of the gunshot ricocheting from the mountains. But he never fired the shot, he never pulled the trigger, and I never saw or spoke to him again until a hiker found his corpse, filthy, naked, emaciated like an ascetic, like a prophet straight from hell, his pitiful remains half-eaten by a wild animal that crawled away to some dark corner and died from the poison that his blood had surely become. And when I learned that he was dead, when, with my own arms, I lowered his coffin into a pit in the local cemetery, watched only by the gravedigger whose help I had declined out of the same foolish pride I had inherited from my father, during a torrent so intense it seemed the sky had ripped in two, and I fell to my knees at the edge of the pit, so devastated was I by what he was taking with him to the grave: the memory of my mother, which he somehow kept alive, over which he stood guard like Cerberus while for me, her face had already begun to fade, the endless hours spent at Les Roches, my loathsome, agonizing initiation to life as he saw it, as the world, as fate had forced him to see it, his unwavering defiance. All these things that had carried on existing far from me, up here in the mountains, like something we think is safely buried, he now took with him. It was as I knelt by the grave in the downpour that I swore to myself that I would finish rebuilding Les Roches, finish the work we had started together, not realizing that some memories are better left dormant, some men better left buried. Because, actually, they're simply waiting for someone to come and dredge them from their deep torpor, so that they can resurface and endlessly repeat the same failures, the same disasters.'

The father stares at the gun in his hands, feels memories, words, images rising to the surface, a blistering confusion of magma. But he says nothing more. He holds his tongue and allows a silent voice to pour out, a deluge from a corner of his consciousness, a vast shadow that hovers over father and son in the sweltering, remorseless glare of summer.

He places the still-warm barrel in his mouth, tastes metal and gunpowder on his tongue, and closes his eyes. The son rushes over, grabs his arms and begs him to put down the gun, but the father is much stronger than the child, his arms do not yield, and he pulls the trigger. A dull click, he opens his eyes, looks at the son and gives a booming laugh, with the barrel of the gun still clenched between his teeth with a broken incisor.

Standing in front of him, the son seems about to burst into tears as the father stows the revolver in the backpack, still laughing, a laugh underscored by a howl, a howl that has come from another time, another reality, another life.

'Got you that time,' he says. 'It was just a joke. At least now I know you'll never leave me.'

◆

After the father's departure, the mother takes on a series of odd jobs to support herself and her son. For several months, she drops him off at dawn at a neighbour's house at the end of the street, and he spends the few hours till morning in a sleeping bag, on a fleecy play rug, next to a baby's cot that smells of dirty nappies and baby lotion.

The neighbour, who answers to the name Livia, is a little Portuguese woman with dark skin and jet-black hair that she keeps shiny with olive oil and egg yolks, who smells of cleansing lotion and talcum powder. Livia is married to a truck driver, Alberto, a gentle, melancholy man who looks to be twice her height and five times her weight. The boy only sees him very occasionally when he is not on the road, sitting in front of the television in a deep armchair whose leather has taken on the smell of the Português Suave cigarettes he smokes. Even the living room is too cramped for him; when he moves about the rooms, which are identical to those in the house the son shares with his mother, he looks as though he is trying to get out without accidentally knocking down a partition wall with his shoulder.

An hour before the school bell rings, Livia wakes the child and gives him breakfast – three buttered biscottes with strawberry jam and a steaming bowl of hot chocolate which forms a thick skin he finds revolting and which she scoops out and savours, criticizing him for having no taste.

The biscottes at the bottom of the bowl turn to a mush that Livia forces him to eat by saying, whenever he sets the bowl down, to eat it all up and put the bowl in the sink. Her home, unlike the mother's, is always spick and span, and smells of lino sluiced with bleach, the O'Cedar wax that makes her furniture shine, the bunches of sage she burns to mask the tenacious smell of Alberto's Português Suave and the pots endlessly simmering on the gas stove.

After breakfast, back when he is six or seven, Livia tells him to undress and, in the cramped bathroom with green tiles coming halfway up the wall, he stands in front of her, his hands covering his genitals as she rubs a soapy, rose-scented flannel over his face, back and his armpits. She scrubs vigorously, seeming satisfied only when his back and arms are red.

All the while, she talks about this and that, about the soap opera she watched the night before – she recounts what happened to the characters with the same emotion as if they were happening to someone she knew – about her childhood in Porto, the houses along the banks of the Douro, their red and ochre façades flushed by the evening light, her mother's house, always cool and shady and smelling of the spices of chorizos curing in the scullery.

The boy loves Livia's conscientious roughness, her languid accent, her attention to detail. After he dresses, she takes a little Roja Flore brilliantine and slicks back his red hair and sometimes, if he asks, dabs his cheeks and wrists with Alberto's woody aftershave.

Upstairs, in an old mahogany cabinet, Livia keeps religious relics, little icons she has brought back from Fátima, holy figurines, translucent plastic Virgin Marys filled with holy water from Lourdes.

Hers is a very idiosyncratic notion of religion, she never sets foot inside a church and she swears in Portuguese '*cabrão de Deus!*' whenever she stubs her foot on a piece of furniture, but she prays at the drop of a hat, prays to Saint Anthony of Padua when she loses a bunch of keys and to Saint Christopher to ensure her husband's safe travels.

As the boy curiously peers into the display case, she describes the origin of each object over and over, the stories varying according to the whims of memory and inspiration.

She slides back the glass panel, the cabinet exhaling a smell of polished wood and incense, picks up one of the Virgins, unscrews her blue plastic crown and sprinkles water onto the palm of her hand, begins to trace the sign of the cross on the child's forehead with her thumb, then changes her mind and pats the holy water on his face. Before replacing the Virgin's crown, she invites him to drink a little, then brings the trepanned skull of the saint to her own lips and swallows a mouthful, as though savouring a precious liqueur. She then refills the Virgin from the tap, convinced that the replenished contents are blessed by dint of proximity.

Among the religious trinkets is a luminous Christ, hanging limply on His plywood cross, that fascinates the child. He asks Livia if he can take a closer look. She holds the statue under a glowing bulb for a few minutes, then allows the boy to lock himself in the small broom closet in the hall. There, in the darkness of the cupboard that smells of cleaning products, in the dim light that creeps under the door behind which Livia is waiting, he contemplates the ghostly figure he is holding, which radiates a greenish phosphorescence, like those deep-sea creatures that light up the darkness with their fearful aura.

Some nights, in a sudden burst of enthusiasm, the mother will say that she is going out with a girlfriend. She gets dressed up, puts on her make-up, sprays a cloud of perfume from the dregs of a bottle of Shalimar, which stinks up the whole house. Her bedroom, usually as much the son's territory as it is hers, is magically transformed by the mother's ritual preening into a place imbued with a very different femininity that keeps him at bay, invoking as it does charms other than the maternal affection usually reserved for him.

He enters only warily, with the feeling of being admitted to a private space that does not concern him and is not intended for him, a space that reveals an unfamiliar part of her, that sensuality which she must have abandoned but which the child senses in one of the photographs – the one in which her legs are bare and she is laughing as the father pretends to bite her – or on those nights when she playfully flirts and simpers in front of him, a simple rehearsal that foreshadows the nights when she intends to flirt 'for real'.

When she goes out, she brings him over to Livia's and, if Alberto is away on business, she stays for a while, and the two women share a glass of wine in the kitchen after they've settled the son in front of the television. Sitting in the deep armchair that gives off a dusty exhalation of Português Suave as he settles himself, he can hear the women's knowing voices from the next room beneath the chatter of the television, the whispered conversations they are careful to keep secret, lowering their voices or suddenly falling silent when he appears in the kitchen, driven by his curiosity or by the fear that his mother will leave without letting him know, without kissing him on the forehead as she usually does, according to their tacit rules.

On occasion, he has walked in to find the mother wiping away tears and Livia leaning over to comfort her about some heartache of which he knows nothing and which, like her earlier titivations, lead him to suspect that different personas coexist in her, or that perhaps she is leading a parallel life to the one they share, just as it is difficult for him to imagine that she was ever a child, a young girl and a woman before she was his mother.

'Cheer up, my love,' he hears Livia say, 'that's all in the past, forget about it, you deserve better. Go out, have fun, take your mind off things.'

They send him back to watch television on the pretext that they are talking about things that don't concern him, and he grudgingly obeys, with the feeling of being banished, of being excluded from grown-up secrets and the complicity of women.

◆

As they draw near Les Roches, they see the mother in the distance, pacing up and down outside the shadowy house that nestles in the lush green of the meadow like a rocky outcrop, an excrescence of stone beneath the slow, indifferent movement of the clouds in the azure sky, sparse, ragged, liable to dissolve at any moment.

She is scanning the horizon and, as soon as she sees them, she quickly approaches through the shimmering light. She walks, runs a few metres, only to be forced to walk by her swollen belly. The son's instinct is to run to her but the father lays a restraining hand on his shoulder. They slow their pace as she approaches. She does not take the path lined with nettles and cuts across the field. A listless breeze ripples the grass, giving the meadow a liquid, undulating appearance. Further away, at the edge of the forest, the swaying leaves alternately reveal their emerald faces and their grey undersides, as the foliage is shaken by a silent tremor.

As she draws nearer, they see her defeated face, her anguished eyes looking from father to son, from son to father, while around them all is still, but for a slow, languorous vibration that might be called epidermal, since it seems to disturb only the surface of the grass, the trees, the observable reality, while the heart of the forest and the stony depths of the mountain remain frozen in hieratic indifference, and the sight of the mother painfully struggling up the steep meadow towards them, moving through this landscape transfigured by the sun, reminds the son of the reproduction of the painting by Andrew Wyeth pasted to a sheet of cardboard, hanging in a clip-frame on the bedroom wall of the cramped house in the town.

When she reaches them, she grabs the boy under the arms and lifts him off the ground.

'Where have you been?' she says. 'I heard gunshots. I was worried sick.'

'It's fine. We just did a little target practice with some bottles.'

In a protective gesture, the reflex of a she-wolf, she cups the child's head and feels the swelling on the back of his skull.

'What happened? Did he hurt himself?'

'He took a bit of a knock, it's nothing, he's fine.'

The mother shakes her head in stunned disbelief.

'You are never to put a gun in that boy's hands again, do you hear?'

'Jesus Christ! Quit mollycoddling the kid, you're doing him no favours.'

'I'm not joking. Don't even think about it.'

Her voice is harsh, quavering, as though daring the father to take the child from her. There is a red spot above her collarbone. The man looks her in the eye, steps closer, deliberately encroaching on her space, soundlessly stamping the grass with his foot as he might shoo a dog or dare it to bite him.

The mother backs away, gripping the child more tightly.

'Don't come near me. Don't come near us.'

She is still backing away, steeling herself to push him at any moment.

He stands, frozen, one foot planted on the ground in front of him, and only when she feels he is out of reach does she turn to take the son back to the house, with the same awkwardly hurried gait that saw her climb the meadow moments earlier, occasionally glancing over her shoulder to make sure the father is not following.

She struggles to carry the boy as she cuts a path through the lush grass, trampling the tall blades that quiver when she has passed, springing back as they attempt to recover their perpendicularity, to make good their rout.

The father watches as she rushes back to Les Roches, the child's head on her shoulder, his arms wrapped around her neck, until finally they reach the shadow of the barn.

He stands, unmoving, unblinking, statuesque, like a scruffy, menacing scarecrow abandoned in the middle of a field, like a farmer in one of the black-and-white photographs documenting country life in the early years of the last century, standing stock-still, solemn and serious in the blazing day, wearing crudely made clothes of dark fabric, rough-hewn muddy wooden clogs, unaccustomed to being photographed, staring into the lens, their weathered faces, their stern eyes sometimes shaded by the brim of a straw hat, which now makes them look as funereal as crows pecking at a recently tilled field.

The summer becomes erratic, alternating days of stifling heat when the mountain is irradiated by white-hot sun, and days of leaden skies of a mineral grey that seems fashioned from strata of coloured silica.

Dotted around the clearings, the flowers of the lizard orchid with their coiled purple labella give off a musky scent in the languid afternoon heat.

Butterflies drunk on pollen flit from one corolla to the next, and, with the help of a book on local fauna he found in his parents' room, the son learns to recognize and identify them: the purple emperor with its reflections of iridescent blue – when he manages to capture one to study the eye-spots on its wings, the insect leaves a greasy powder on his fingertips – the Duke of Burgundy with its chalklike markings, and the orange tip with its flaming forewings.

He is fascinated by the mystery of their Latin names – *Apatura iris, Hamearis lucina, Anthocharis cardamines, Argynnis paphia, Aglais io* – which, he senses, harbour the secrets of these bodies so fragile that they are carried in the wind and apt to crumble to dust, the profound reason for these lives, so fleeting and foreign yet parallel to his own, living in the same world, but on another plane, another reality.

Though he usually finds studying difficult and rebarbative, he effortlessly memorizes the names and recites them to himself as fervently as if they were mantras, lines snatched from an epic poem whose meaning had been lost.

If insects – so distant yet so close – are what he loves most, he also marvels at the common names of the birds that live in the mountains, their vibrating presence, their multiple, inexhaustible voices: the blackcap, the bullfinch, the serin, the owl of Minerva, the northern goshawk.

In the evening, as the sky flushes purple, he watches stag beetles rise from the shadowy forest, where their larvae have spent up to six years buried beneath the trunks of ancient oaks, before the droning imago takes to the wing and flies off in search of a mate, drinking sap from sickly trees beneath which the females will soon bury their eggs.

Everything that surrounds him offers the child a glimpse of the endless cycle of unhurried life, governed by enigmatic laws whose mysteries envelop him as he lingers, grows familiar, and melts into them.

In the days following the confrontation with the father, the mother is once again laid low by one of the usual migraines that have given her a little respite since they came up to Les Roches. Confined to bed, she lies in the bedroom with the shutters closed. As the hours pass, the band of sunlight that slips between the shutters sweeps across the walls and ceiling; she does her best to avoid it when it moves across the bed, groaning and seeking refuge, on one side or another of the mattress.

The son, a seasoned home nurse, stays by her side; he soaks the flannel in the basin of cool water and wrings it out before laying it on her forehead wreathed with menthol vapours; he holds the plastic basin when she is sick. Meanwhile, the father, unaccustomed to these episodes or forced to accept her order to stay away from her and the child, crosses the threshold reluctantly now that the house is home only to the mother's sufferings, to the sorrowful chiaroscuro constrained by the closed shutters.

He mooches around, mulishly silent, a Marlboro smouldering at the corner of his mouth. He begins to clear the ruined outbuildings, sorts and stacks old slates with the idea of replacing the damaged ones on the main roof, feverishly flitting from one task to the next without finishing any.

He tends the kitchen garden, but the sickly, stunted plants offer only a handful of tomatoes that rot before they ripen, small bitter lettuces half-eaten by slugs. Everything defies him, the rocks, the very mountain itself, by some strange force – the mother seeking refuge in her pain – meeting his efforts with a reproachful apathy.

He rises before dawn as the stars begin to pale and falls asleep on the sofa in the early evening, his increasingly gaunt face turned towards the glowing fire.

After four days' rest, the mother reappears on the threshold of the house, letting the now benign morning light warm her body numbed by sleep and painkillers. She looks more fragile than usual, her face is paler, her eyes, glassy from too little sleep, are ringed with dark circles.

The father comes and stands behind her, hugging her as he kisses her neck. He runs a hand over her belly and whispers apologies and tender words in her ear. An enigmatic smile plays on the mother's lips, but she says nothing. Just now, anything seems better than the excruciating agony that had her bedridden a day earlier, and perhaps she is prepared to believe one last time – before the madness of fathers, so long suppressed, this poison passed from generation to generation and, until now, hidden in the depths of the mountain and the hearts of men, falls upon Les Roches – that reconciliation is possible, that they will eventually find peace here and, from then on, everything will be serene.

When they manage to get an FM station on the radio, they hear announcements of the total solar eclipse, the last of the century, which will take place in a few days.

The father tells the son that this is something he should not miss since it will not come again for eighty-two years, by which time the son will be ninety-one.

He warns him not to stare at the sun with the naked eye: 'You could go blind or burn a hole in your eyes.'

He smokes shards of glass from the old windows under a candle flame until the soot forms a thick layer. He rubs the sharp edges smooth with sandpaper, then tells the boy to hold one of the shards and look at the sun.

'It's not perfect,' he says, 'but it'll do.'

The child closes his left eye, and peers through the thick blackened glass with his right, the sun's orb condensed into a luminous disc with perfectly defined contours, the sun tamed.

Later, remembering the father's words, the son is overwhelmed by the fear of blindness, just as he was on the night they arrived at Les Roches, when he woke up in the pitch-dark bedroom to the unfamiliar sounds of the house and the mountain.

Yet he cannot help but ignore the father's advice and raise his face to the sky to defy the star for as long as possible. As soon as he feels his cornea burn, he looks away as the afterimage of a black sun still floats in his field of vision.

Terrified at the idea that he has burned a hole in his eyes and not daring to tell his father that he disobeyed him, he runs to the forest and seeks refuge in the hollow among the roots of the old walnut tree, where he cries for a long time before finally falling asleep, the dark spectre still floating behind his closed eyelids.

When he wakes, his sight has been restored. A salamander in a damp, dark crevice is staring with its pupilless eyes of pure black obsidian.

On the day of the eclipse, they sit in front of the house, holding the smoked shards of glass. The sky is ash-grey, though here and there steep shafts of sunlight rake the earth.

'We're not going to be able to see anything,' the father says disappointedly.

A bated breath moves over the mountain. It is the mother who first notices the sudden silence around them as the light dwindles and the shadows turn blue.

'Listen,' she says to the son, 'the birds have stopped singing.'

Then the skies part, a rush of light momentarily dispels the darkness, setting the treetops ablaze before a shadow takes its place.

Together they raise the shards of glass and watch as the sun is engulfed by the black disc of the moon. The vault of the heavens takes shape, darkness spreads across the earth and a crepuscular humidity rises from the earth.

As she watches the sun disappear, devoured by the body of the moon, the mother feels a familiar, dull anguish well inside her again, a looming sense of tragedy like the one she felt when she saw the father slashing at the vegetable garden, or in the recurring dream about the swing when she knew the son was about to have an accident.

A tightness in her chest leaves her breathless and she turns away from the eclipse. For a moment, the world is plunged into twilight, a baleful, slate-blue, sepulchral penumbra whose density consumes and suffocates her.

She drops the piece of blackened glass and rushes off. Gasping for air, she pounds her chest with her fist and squeezes her eyes shut so as not to have to see the desolate mountain consumed by purple bruises.

The father doesn't notice her absence. When he turns away from the eclipse, he sees her standing, frozen in the grass, about ten metres away, her head bowed, as though in prayer.

'What's the matter?' he asks, walking over to her.

She shakes her head and looks at him, distraught.

'It's the baby,' she says in a whisper so that the son will not overhear. 'I think something's wrong.'

'What's wrong?'

'I don't know. It's hard to explain. It's just a feeling.'

The moon breaks free of the sun and light once more bursts forth from a precise point in the dark mass.

From behind them, the boy shouts:

'The sun's coming out again! Look!'

The father glances at the son.

'There's no reason why everything shouldn't go well,' he says. 'You just need to get some rest.'

'I think I should see someone, a doctor.'

The father runs his tongue over his teeth, lays an appeasing hand on the mother's arm.

'I'm sure you're worrying about nothing. Let's leave it for a few days. If you still feel the same then, we'll go home, okay?'

'We could always come back later,' says the mother.

The father shakes his head, brings his hand up to rest on her cheek.

'If we leave, we leave for good, you know that. I'm just asking you to wait a little. It's not a decision we should make on the spur of the moment.'

He runs his thumb across her lips and holds it there, silencing her, as day breaks over them once more. The son runs over to them while the mother, slowly, imperceptibly, nods.

Late summer stretches out in a mesmerizing slowness, languid nights when even the stones of Les Roches exude their moisture, sun-scorched days, nebulous, surreal dawns abruptly slashed by the blade of the day, furnace-red sunsets that, a moment later, dwindle to purple shadows, to charcoal blacks.

The mother no longer goes with the son on his expeditions. Since the day of the eclipse, she has surrendered to mute resignation, drifting upon dark waters where neither child nor father can reach her. She is present with them, her body moves, albeit with a palpable slowness, she talks to them, but she has taken refuge in some recess of her soul that keeps her at a distance.

She spends long hours wandering around Les Roches without ever straying further, sometimes smoking with a faint air of disgust – only when he sees the cigarette in her mouth does the son realize that she stopped smoking some weeks ago – engrossed in a lengthy inner conversation, her weary gaze moves over the objects before her without really seeing them; or she lies in the room, her swollen belly forcing her to stay on her side, and watches the degrees of daylight move across the walls.

Alert to the sudden strangeness of the mother, the son constantly keeps her in his field of vision when not simply staying by her side. He tries to entertain her with stories he makes up, games she sometimes plays reluctantly, but more often refuses on the pretext that she needs to rest.

He brings her blackberries from outside, which he accidentally crushes on his way, purpling his palms, and little objects that end up cluttering the dark green metal canteen: stones of curious shapes or colours, snake skins, bleached bones gleaned from the edge of a burrow, driftwood, a robin's egg the colour of agate . . . She gratefully eats the berries one by one; she keeps the little treasures, gazing at them as though they were brought to her from some far-flung world, from a reality now beyond her reach, or as though they are relics of a bygone era.

* * *

But still the child continues to visit the horses. Their quiet, unresponsive presence is a counterpoint to that of the mother and father. As he walks into the clearing, the horses raise their heads, the foal or one of the mares neighs gently.

The boy cleans the stallion's empty eye-socket, runs his fingers over the dent above the animal's eye and its gaunt flanks. He imagines staying here with them, not going back to Les Roches. After all, children have been raised by wolves. But that would mean leaving the mother to the tender mercies of the father, so in the end he always decides to return home.

During the time, however brief, that he spends dozing on the grass next to the horses, he imagines himself galloping with them, having no needs, no hopes, beyond the serene freedom, the mysterious, disjointed temporality of the mountain, where things have no beginning or end, where they seem always to have been what they are and to be in no danger of extinction.

After dark one night – a colder, damper night that carries within it the indolent promise of autumn – while the son is watching the stars wheel in the sky, the father comes and sits next to him.

'What was the third time?' says the son.

'The third time?'

'Your father. You said he used the revolver three times.'

'Oh,' says the father. 'Well, you remember the fox I told you about? The one I had up here at Les Roches.'

'Yes.'

The father admits that he wasn't telling the truth when he said he didn't remember what happened to the fox cub. It was the father who found the animal when it was barely weaned, and from that first moment, the fox cub trusted the boy with the absolute trust that animals place in those who have saved them. Before long, says the father, the fox became the centre of his world, his only friend, living, sleeping and playing with him, until a day came when the old man found the presence of the fox cub intolerable, perhaps because he thought the animal was overshadowing him or distracting the son from his chores.

'How can I possibly know what was going through his mind?'

The father says that the old man took a sudden dislike to the fox cub, came to almost hate it, he claimed that sooner or later it would bite the boy or give him some disease, and so one night, while the child was sleeping, he took the fox cub and left it out in the forest, probably miles from Les Roches. But this was to underestimate the ability animals here on earth have of finding their way, because the fox came back.

'There he sat, trembling at the door in the early hours of the morning, his soft fur spattered with mud and tangled with twigs and thorns.'

Once, twice, three times the fox came back, probably guided by a sense of smell or some sixth sense beyond the understanding of men. And it was on the third time that the father had seen the old man wield the revolver, as he took a large canvas bag into which he stuffed the struggling fox cub, already aware of the fate that awaited him this time, a fate from which he would not escape. As the old man walked off, the boy clung to his trousers, let himself be dragged across the ground, stubbornly pulling on the leg, but had not managed to stop him. When his hands could no longer keep a grip on the bony shin, he let go.

'I lay there, face down in the grass, screaming and pounding my fists on the soft earth until I heard a shot ring out in the mountain. I knew it was over, that I would never see the fox cub again.'

The boy had rolled over onto his back, his anger abruptly crushed, it having become so unbearable that it had collapsed in on itself, leaving nothing but a feeling of strangeness, of numbness. The father said that he waited without a word for the old man to return, to pass by carrying the canvas bag, now empty, with a bullet hole in the side, stained with the fox cub's blood and, leaving him there, walk on, whistling as if he had just performed a necessary, not particularly unpleasant task, and was congratulating himself on a job well done, and, in killing the fox, on having re-established a sense of order according to rules that he alone understood.

Engrossed in other thoughts, the father brings a cigarette to his lips. The flame of the lighter glows blue in the darkness. He jabs at the sky with the burning cigarette and explains to the son that the human eye can see only a small part of the sky, a section so insignificant that we have no conception of what the heavens really are.

There are other stars, he says, other planets, some so dark that no sun ever reaches them, and beyond that, there are other galaxies, thousands of them, and each galaxy contains billions of suns, billions of planets, and beyond everything that is visible, he says, there are hundreds of billions of galaxies.

'Are there other earths like ours?'

'I hope not,' says the father after a prolonged silence. 'I hope there's nothing. Nothing but rock, silence, ice and fire.'

◆

One night, coming home from work, the mother steps through the door and the roar of men laughing in the living room hits her in the chest. She stands, motionless, in the usually pleasant and welcoming half-light of the hallway, illuminated by an amber glow that filters through the glass panels of the door.

She takes off her coat, hangs it on a hook and stares at her reflection in the mirror hanging on the wall; her face is drawn and tired, her hair carelessly held up by one of the elastic ties she sometimes wears around her wrist, absentmindedly twisting it between her fingers until it frays.

She tries to put on a brave face, to banish the mingled fear and exhaustion that have abruptly reshaped her features in the crepuscular hallway, but she is not startled, nor even faintly surprised, since she knows what is waiting for her when she moves into the nimbus of light and smoke from which come the coarse overlapping voices of men chatting with a friendliness that is too jaunty to be entirely sincere. Doubtless, she has secretly steeled herself for this, resigned and prepared herself, knowing that at any moment the father could summon up the ghost that is Tony – or, rather, the ghost of what the three of them once were, of what they meant to one another, and to everyone else: a trio alternately envied, hated or scorned – knowing that the father would inevitably summon Tony, and perhaps even that his return has no other purpose beyond reuniting them, forcing them to face each other.

And as she walks towards the rectangle of light made denser by the smoke from their cigarettes, the radiant heat of their alcoholic breath and their voices in chorus in the cramped living room, she has already adopted a mask of unruffled geniality, of charming detachment that she feels might crack and fall apart at any moment.

'Tony,' she says from the doorway.

'Hey,' says Tony, turning to look at her.

He makes as if to stand, only to sit back down under the triumphant glare of the father, who stubs his cigarette out on the rim of one of the empty beer cans on the coffee table.

'Look who's dropped round to see us.'

The mother flashes a quick smile.

'Where's the boy?' she asks.

'Up in his room, I assume,' says the father with barely disguised disinterest.

Then, with renewed enthusiasm:

'Why didn't you tell me Tony had two kids!'

The mother says nothing. Since the father's return, they have never talked about Tony. His name has never even been mentioned, though it burned on the tips of their tongues – for one, an imprecation, for the other, a blasphemy – and all the while it was the presence, the idea of Tony that hovered over them, rather than the reality of flesh and blood – his coexistence, in the same town, only a few kilometres away – snatches of the past they had shared with him. The keen, heart-wrenching memory of gestures made, words spoken, of the years buried after the father's departure, relegated to the limbo of a life that, to all of them, feels like a previous existence, and which has nonetheless brought them together in the hazy, comforting glow of the ceiling light in the living room of a little house in a run-down district, where they seem to be trying in vain to reenact one of those scenes in which they used to appear together, inseparable.

'Twins,' says the father, 'can you believe it?'

'Yes.'

'He showed me a photo. Tony, show her the photo.'

Tony stands, frozen, a rueful smile on his face, staring intently at the beer can in his hands, as though the father's words had not reached him.

'Tony, show her the photo,' says the father, now brooking no argument.

Stung by the father's insistence, Tony gets to his feet with guilty rapidity, betraying a submissiveness of which he seeks to absolve himself in the mother's eyes with an apologetic smile. He reaches into the back pocket of his jeans, takes out a wallet and nervously rummages through it for the photograph.

The mother steps forward, takes the photograph and for a moment she stares at a young woman whose face bears the tell-tale dark blotches of pregnancy mask, cradling two chubby babies.

'Two little boys,' says the father, whose eyes she can feel boring into her. 'They look just like her, don't they?'

'Yes, just like her,' says the mother.

'And his little wife, isn't she pretty?'

'Very pretty.'

'That's Sylvia, do you recognize her? You remember Sylvia, don't you? She was the eldest of the Legendre girls, the ones who . . .'

'Of course. I remember Sylvia,' the mother interrupts him.

'Of course,' repeats the father. 'Of course, you know her.'

'I think I'll head off,' says Tony, slipping the photo back into his wallet.

The father also gets to his feet, raises his eyes to meet Tony's, their bodies separated only by the width of the coffee table, casting long shadows on the walls – that's how they've always been, the mother thinks, opposite poles.

'We haven't seen each other for ages, do you really think I'm going to let you go just like that? Why don't you stay and have dinner with us?'

'Thanks,' says Tony, 'the thing is, I didn't realize how late it was. I should be home by now. Sylvia will be waiting.'

The father laughs, his tone dry and mocking.

'Give her a call, I'm sure she'll understand.'

'Drop it,' says the mother. 'He's just told you she's home alone with two small children . . .'

'But I don't want to drop it!' roars the father, grabbing Tony's shoulder and squeezing it. 'You're staying for dinner, end of story.'

Tony nods and the father flashes the mother a triumphant smile.

'Fine,' she says. 'I'm going up to change.'

'Go on then, go,' he says, playfully shooing her away. 'We'll see to dinner.'

She goes upstairs, stops in front of the son's room and glances at him through the half-open door. Lying on his back on the carpet, the boy is holding a Masters of the Universe action figure bought for ten francs at one of the annual rummage sales held in a local schoolyard; he is whispering stories to this blue-skinned character wearing a purple cowl and breastplate, with a grinning yellow skull for a face.

The mother knocks on the door and the son turns to look.

'I'm just home. Did you have a nice day?'

The son nods. She steps into the room.

'Is something the matter?'

'Are you angry with me?' says the boy.

'Why would I be angry?'

'Because I'm the one who told him about Uncle Tony.'

The mother comes and sits cross-legged on the floor next to him.

'When did you tell him about Uncle Tony?'

'The other day. When we were at the funfair.'

'Was he asking you questions?'

The son nods.

'And what did you tell him?'

'I didn't tell him anything. Just that he comes round and helps out sometimes.'

She gently takes his chin and lifts his face towards her.

'I'm not angry with you,' she says. 'Why are you worried?'

The son shrugs and turns his attention back to the action figure.

'I don't want you worrying. Leave the grown-ups to work things out for themselves, okay? There's no reason for you to worry.'

'Why did he go away?' asks the child. 'And why did he come back?'

'I wish I could explain,' says the mother. 'But there are some things too complicated for a nine-year-old to understand.'

'I'm old enough to understand.'

'Maybe you're right. I hope maybe one day you'll understand. In fact, I'm sure you will. Right, I'm going to take a shower,' she says, getting up. 'We'll be eating soon. Tony is staying for dinner.'

The son does not answer and she lingers for a moment, one hand on the doorframe, watching him make the action figure fly.

In the bathroom, she turns on the shower, then changes her mind, puts the plug in the bath and turns on the tap to drown out the distant rumble of men's voices.

She sits on the edge of the bath, suddenly overcome by exhaustion, her hands resting on the tiles either side of her legs. She sits motionless, staring at the pink bathmat at her feet, lulled by the sound of water gushing around her, and the faintly chlorinated mist of steam that she can feel rising behind her, settling on the delicate hairs on the back of her neck and fogging up the room. Wearily, she takes off her clothes and leaves them on the floor. She stretches her stiff legs, her arms whose every joint aches from performing the same actions all day long.

She slips into the steaming bath so that she can hear only muffled sounds, the clanking of the pipes, the subtle friction of her skin against the enamel bath. She runs a hand over her belly. For two months now, the pregnancy test with its ominous blue line has been lying at the bottom of the blue plastic bin next to the sink where she carefully buried it, relegating the information and its consequences to a remote corner of her mind.

She bends her legs and lets her face slide under the surface. A confusion of images rises up, she hears an inner voice like waves crashing over her memory, her own voice speaking across the years.

She sees the father suddenly reappearing in town, still in his teens, recognized by a few of the local lads, some of whom hung out with him at school before his mother died and he vanished, dragged up into the mountains by his father – for reasons they never knew or no longer remembered – and now sleeping under a duvet on the backseat of a Renault 30 that he had probably bought in a wrecking yard or from some farmer for a wad of cash, and overhauled – God knows how – using spare parts he picked up here and there.

'And he used to drive it, even though he was only seventeen and didn't have a licence.'

This was how he and Uncle Tony had met, tinkering with cars together, spending days poring over stripped-down engines, nights in the glare of floodlights and headlamps down in the inspection pit, forming a little gang with a couple of other mouthy, mindless boys, haunting café pool halls which they filled with smoke and wild roars of laughter, the summer barn dances in neighbouring villages, lurking on the edges of a marquee set up in the church square or the car park of a village hall. They lived in a parallel universe, one where their little gang huddled around cars, keeping the engines revved and the exhausts belching, six-packs of beer sitting on the gleaming bonnets, girls orbiting them like satellites, pining in the arms of one boy or another, sometimes simultaneously.

'Before they disappeared, going back to their dull lives and the dreary town.'

The gang elicited envy or contempt, scoffing at everything, keenly aware of their athletic bodies, stripping down on the riverbanks in summer and hurling themselves from the bridges into pools of limpid water, and in their midst, the father – who was not yet a father, but a child playing at being a man, giddy and idiotically proud at the idea of having become one – the most unknowable, the most unpredictable of them all, the one who seemed to magnetically draw them together and bind them; the wildest too, quick to throw a punch if he thought some guy in a bar had looked at him funny, but watching over his gang with a brotherly, almost tender affection. They would ride into town, a horde of swaggering, hot-tempered young gods who didn't give a shit about rules, about what other people thought, who had a vitality that seemed extraordinarily enviable to the local boys and girls.

They were all fifteen, eighteen, twenty years old, they were all born here, had grown up here and they already knew that most of them would grow old here, trapped in their houses in this one-horse town, trussed and tethered in the hollow of this valley, held in a vice by the mountain, doomed to their fate as the sons and daughters of labourers, warehousemen, welders, quarrymen, caretakers, though some still dreamed of getting out, with the intense, intoxicating feeling that their salvation depended on the greatest distance they could put between themselves and this town.

'At least that's what I longed for. I felt as though, until then, I'd been trapped in life's waiting room, submerged in a stultifying inertia, under the thumb of a mother who was stony, hostile, disapproving.'

And when she was allowed to join the gang, she was desperate to believe in the promise of something else, intoxicated by the father's apparent freedom, his rebelliousness, his lust for life, intoxicated by endless nights, dissolved in the fumes of weed and booze, the smell of white-hot engines, the car races along tricky, treacherous mountain roads.

'Late at night, when he'd suddenly get gloomy and morose, when the booze loosened his tongue and he started to spew his hatred for the town, with that black fire in his eyes, I didn't see it as a threat, but as a promise that sooner or later we'd get out of there, that he'd find a way to get us out.'

But something held him back, perhaps the distant presence of the father he had left up in the mountains, about whom she knew almost nothing, and when the old man died, when two gendarmes came to the door to tell them that the old man's body had been found up there, he had simply nodded, unsurprised, as though he had been expecting the news for a long time. He refused to let anyone go with him when he identified the body, he had probably stood alone, bolt-upright looking at his father's remains in the harsh glare of the mortuary viewing room, and he had also insisted on being alone on the day the old man was laid to rest.

'I remember a heavy rainstorm, the muddy knees of his trousers when he came back, pale, already haunted.'

This was probably when things began to change – or this was what she often thought later, although at first neither of them was aware of the tiny, imperceptible shifts – he simply became quieter, more solemn, his moods even more volatile, and his obsession with racing cars got more intense. But sometimes she would overhear the gang whispering about cars they had to pick up and drive to the border, and she would walk away from these conversations. She didn't want to know, didn't want to think about it. When they went on trips for two or three days, she never asked any questions of them or of herself.

Having moved around between various apartments in the town centre, they settled in a large, half-empty house that they wound up renting with Tony – who had always been the closest, the most devoted member of the gang – where a rowdy procession of the faithful came and went at all hours of the day and night.

'I think maybe I preferred to remain ignorant, the same way I preferred the life we were living, which I still believed was completely carefree and permissive, although it probably never was.'

And when she found out that she was pregnant, she had found the strength within to calm the mounting panic that gripped her; she thought she would be up to the task, that becoming a mother was one way of being fulfilled, of leaving behind the long, excruciating childhood she had thought would never end, that she would become a grown-up and would have no choice but to win her independence and her freedom.

'When I told him, he put his arms around me, kissed my lips, my forehead, my nose, my cheeks a hundred times. "You're going to give me a son," he said over and over, laughing, his eyes filled with tears. I kept telling him I didn't know, he refused to listen, I was going to have his son.'

Never had she seen him happier than that day, and in the weeks and months before and after the birth of his son. But she had not counted on what was dogging him, the something – whatever it was – that he took with him the day he fled from Les Roches, and that had already begun to draw him back.

He began to go back again, initially without telling her, later casually mentioning some maintenance work, just enough to keep the house from falling down, and every time she offered to go with him, he refused, telling her that there was nothing to see, that he would take her there some day when he felt the time was right.

In her eyes, nothing existed anymore beyond the child she had just had, and she did not notice the father becoming more distant, or the emptiness gradually but inexorably developing around him, some of the guys in the gang drifting away, tired of his fits of rage, others cast out, banished from the group over vague disagreements, or because they disapproved of and refused to take part in the 'business deals' that were taking up more and more of his time. One night, a boy of twenty-one drove off the road, smashed through a guardrail and hit a tree at the edge of a gully, and that was the end of the clandestine races. Others had taken up jobs, settled down, married local girls. Without realizing, they had all grown up, and few had left the town.

'The town slammed shut with us inside – that's assuming we ever really had a chance to escape.'

Before the mother's eyes, the father had turned into an impenetrable, quick-tempered, obsessive man whom she now feared. His only remaining ally was Uncle Tony, ever obedient, caught in his trap; reliable old Tony, from whom the mother got the attention, the gentleness, the closeness that the father lacked – not much of a compensation for the dreams she'd nurtured that had turned to dust.

Two years passed in the vast, cold house which he ended up furnishing in an extravagant mismatched fashion, where she spent most of her time wandering alone, cradling her son in her arms, punctuated by occasional fleeting visits from her mother, during which they would sit facing each other, the elderly genetrix with her handbag on her pointedly clenched knees, surveying the room with an air of disapproval and disbelief, as though she had found herself in a particularly uncomfortable, indeed ignominious position, half-heartedly sipping the coffee served her before suddenly asking: 'Is this really what you want? Is this really the way you want to bring up your son?'

'And I would always give a bitter laugh and say, "What do you mean? Are you saying you think your life is better, more respectable, more deserving than mine?"'

Each remained immured in her own silence, the silence of two women who could not bear to see in the other the same disappointment, the same sense of failure and despair. Sometimes the elderly mother would hold the son so tightly that it looked as though she wanted to tear him away from her daughter, to save him from what she doubtless thought was her negligence, her irresponsibility.

'And I sometimes wondered if she was right, which just made her visits even more unbearable.'

Then came the night when the father, who had probably been away for some days, laid a hand on her shoulder, shook her awake and told her that she had to get up and get dressed right now, take everything she and the child possessed and leave, because men would be coming in the morning to take him away, and he did not want her, or the son – young as he was – to be there when they did.

'He said: "Tony will take you to your mother's place," and I didn't ask him to explain because it would have been useless, I got up without a word, I did what he told me, I took a small suitcase packed with whatever was to hand, because I didn't give a shit if I forgot something, in fact I felt it might be better for us to leave everything behind, because I felt mute resentment towards him welling up inside me, a rage that had been building for so long that it had congealed in my gut, forming this hard, burning knot that felt like it would rip me open.'

The father was nearby but at a distance, watching as she randomly stuffed the suitcase with some clothes, a photo album and a few trinkets – the things a person takes when they're running away, with that dreadful feeling of humiliation. He stood in the corner of the room, stiff and solemn, but sheepish too, staring at his feet, like a bewildered teenager and, at the same time, like a disillusioned old man, and when the mother had finished packing, they stood facing each other, she with the suitcase in one hand and her son in the other.

'"Take good care of him," he said, and he kissed me on the corner of the lips, an overattentive kiss I avoided by turning away, "take good care of him until I get back." "Until you get back," I repeated with all the contempt I could muster.'

Then she had walked out of that house and did not hear from the father again until the day he decided to come back into their lives, and in the meantime she retained only a haunting memory of the years they had spent together, a bitter nostalgia, the conviction that if he ever did come back, she would know how to refuse him the forgiveness she imagined him begging for.

'How many times did I imagine pushing him away, how many times did I play out the scene where I rejected him, and how many times have I felt my heart implode when I thought I saw him on a street corner?'

But when she had seen him lying in her room, as though sleeping the sleep of the just, it brought back all the shared moments that she had shut away, pushed to the back of her mind, and all the rage she had nurtured, all the resentment she had endlessly rehashed suddenly crumbled, swept away by a rekindled hope that surfaced from her previous life, that perhaps they could be together, reunited.

Now, in the warm embrace of the bath, her mind wanders to the muted rhythm of her heart, where space and time do not exist; she feels it might be possible, even desirable to dissolve in the warmth that surrounds and cradles her, to be taken away from the world, from the presence of the father, of Tony, even of the son: relieved of the burden of their respective holds on her.

Could she not simply disappear?

She sits up, splashing water on the tiled floor, and for a moment she sits with one hand held to the edge of the bath and the other on her breast.

The father has set the living room table, fried up a mess of frozen green beans, minced beef and potatoes and taken cans of cold beer from the fridge. He now seems to be quietly cheerful, rejoicing in Tony's brotherly presence, and Tony too seems noticeably relaxed, no longer dreading the reprisals that seemed to lurk beneath the father's genial manner.

They both eat heartily and talk openly. The father wants to know everything about Tony's life, about the years since they were last in touch: what jobs has he had, given that his only talent was as a mechanic, how long has he been working in electronics, does he earn a decent living, how did he and Sylvia get together, where do they live now, how does he feel about fatherhood?

He listens to Tony's answers with an impatience perceptible only to the mother, his eyes constantly dart towards her, making sure she's aware of the life Tony has built without her, and she is content to listen to them talk, though she cannot quite shake off the sense of mistrust, of dread at the prospect of her own annihilation that had gripped her earlier in the bathroom.

To relieve her anxiety, she gets up, lights a Peter Stuyvesant and goes to open the window to let some air into the room. The son brings her an orange, sits on the sofa and starts flicking through an old TV guide. She smokes for a while, watching the roofs of the houses sink into the darkness, peels the orange and hands the segments to the boy.

Leaning back in his chair, the father brings a Marlboro to his lips.

'Do you remember the Lancia Thema 8.32?'

'Are you kidding?' says Tony, taking a cigarette from the pack the father is holding out.

He leans over the flame of the Zippo, which exudes the smell of lighter fluid.

'Of course I remember it – Ferrari V8 engine, leather seats, walnut dashboard.'

'And the Mercedes 500E? Now, that thing could really move,' says the father, his eyes shining. 'Remember the night we drove her all the way to Spain? We had two cop cars chasing us.'

'Go brush your teeth and put on your pyjamas,' the mother tells the son. 'Give Uncle Tony a kiss.'

'Five thousand ccs of raw power, zero to a hundred in six seconds! I nearly got 250 kilometres per hour out of her on the motorway.'

Tony offers his cheek and the boy kisses it.

'I'll be up to say goodnight in fifteen minutes,' says the mother as the child reluctantly leaves the living room.

'While the fucking cops were trying to shift into second to get onto the motorway, we were already leaving at the next exit,' said the father, laughing. 'How much did we make on it again?'

'On the Merc? Ten grand, fifteen grand, I don't remember. Cars like that were selling for forty K cash in hand.'

'Those were the days. You can say what you like, but those were the good days. When I think of the piece of shit I drive now.'

Tony shakes his head and they puff on their cigarettes, lost in thought.

The mother tears the orange peel into tiny shreds and puts them on her plate.

'Do I have to remind you that they were pretty short-lived, the good days?' she says to the father.

'If the Gypsy hadn't ratted me out, we would have made a shitload of cash.'

'It's all a long time ago,' says Tony.

Abruptly, the mother clears the table and disappears into the kitchen. The men can hear the clatter of plates in the sink and the sound of running water.

'I'm gonna tell you something,' says the father, leaning over and whispering to Tony, 'we never should have trusted those spics, we should never have agreed to be gofers. We were fucking dumb. We shoulda had more ambition.'

'Come on! We barely knew how to change a number plate and get across the border. Refitting, respraying and selling, that was all down to the Gypsy.'

'Yeah, but we could have got a bit more involved, made a bit more cash. That fucker made a huge wedge off our work.'

'He came a cropper in the end, and so did the spics. We would have ended up going down for something else, it was only a matter of time.'

'But you didn't go down, did you, Tony? You fell through the cracks,' the father says, his voice suddenly toneless as he stares at Tony over the beer he is holding to his mouth.

He sets the can back on the table and says:

'You could have, but I never grassed you up.'

'I know,' says Tony. 'And I'm grateful.'

The father nods and says nothing. The mother reappears in the doorway.

'I'm going to bed,' she says. 'I'm tired.'

'Tony's just about to leave,' the father says, getting to his feet without ever taking his eyes off Tony. 'I'll see him home.'

The two men walk out into the cold, yellow night of the yard.

'One for the road?' says the father, proffering his packet of cigarettes.

Tony pulls up the collar of his jacket and waves the pack away.

'Thanks, I've smoked too much already, I'm trying to quit.'

'Really?'

'Now we've got the kids, Sylvia thinks it's for the best.'

The father inhales a thick cloud of smoke and the two men silently stare at the glistening flagstones, breathing in the familiar smells of the run-down neighbourhood.

'Ah, Tony, Tony, Tony, my old mate,' says the father.

He punches Tony in the shoulder, a slow firm punch, forcing him to take a step back. Tony gives a little snigger.

'It was good to see you again,' says the father. 'But now we have to get a few things clear.'

'Like what?' says Tony with a diffident laugh.

'I don't ever want to see you set foot in this house again,' said the father. 'I don't even want to see you come through this gate, walk down this street, or any other street in the neighbourhood.'

'What are you talking about?'

'I don't want you anywhere near my wife or my son. I don't want to see your back-stabbing face in this town ever again. And if you ever see me, if you ever see any of us, please turn away. Turn away and get the fuck out as fast as you can.'

In the gloom of the porch, Tony swallows hard, the father steps closer and gives him a long hug, then takes his face in his hands and kisses his forehead.

'Because I'm afraid I won't be responsible for my actions,' he says in a soft, sorrowful voice. 'Do you get what I'm saying? I'm afraid I'll hurt you, Tony. I'm afraid I might kill you.'

In the father's hands, Tony's face is ashen, his left eyelid twitches and he nods.

'Now, fuck off,' the father commands.

He goes into the bedroom, sits at the foot of the bed and, with slow drunken movements, he undresses, his back turned to the mother who is careful not to move so that he will think she is asleep. But he starts talking to her in a deep, slurred, toneless voice. He says that he expects her to give him another chance. That maybe she wondered why he was never in touch during the years he was gone, the reasons for him coming home. He says that there was no point writing, that sometimes a man needs to know how to be humble, to be modest, to spare those close to him from his disgrace. In the same way that certain animals have the presence of mind, the tact – the nobility even – to go off and hide when they realize that they are injured or dying, and their weakness might harm those around them. If he has come back now, it is because he expects her, the mother, to give him another chance, because he has come to claim his right to once again be considered as a partner and as a father.

From the tone of his voice, she knows that this is not a request. He is merely telling her that she has no choice but to give him what he has come back to demand from them. And though she has not planned it, has made no move that would let the father know that she has been listening, she says in a barely audible voice:

'I'm pregnant.'

He sits, frozen, though she could swear she sees him sway in the waxen glow pouring through the window onto the bedspread.

'Is it Tony's?'

'What difference does it make,' she says. 'What difference does it make?'

'None, I suppose.'

He gets up, wearing only a pair of white briefs, walks around the bed and lets himself topple onto his back next to her, like a felled tree. For interminable minutes he lies silently in the yellow half-light.

'Do you remember Les Roches?'

She nods in the darkness.

He tells her that long ago he set about restoring the house with no clear goal other than to honour his father's memory in some way, but that before he came back to the town, he went up to the mountains to carry on the work, this time with the idea that mother and son would live there with him, that only in doing so can the three of them find each other again; that their stay will be their new start.

His voice is quavering with emotion. He gropes for her hand on the sheet and squeezes it the way a child might.

'Give me this chance,' he says. 'Let me prove to you that I've changed.'

◆

At the end of August, a storm hits Les Roches.

The father, mother and the son are asleep when an inky blackness, thicker than night, masses in the sky, criss-crossed from time to time by spasms of lightning that reveal the tops of the huge clouds.

In the father's dream, the old man is piling up the stones of a ruin he is struggling to build – the father knows it is Les Roches, but the pile of rubble next to him is abnormally vast, as though a massive edifice once stood there, a castle, a fortress – the wall he is constructing is slapdash, and at any moment might collapse and bury him. The father is unsure whether to shout a warning, but the thought that the old man might become aware of his presence fills him with a profound revulsion, he thinks: what am I so scared of, since he's already dead and this is just a dream? In the same moment he realizes that the fear is not about the old man coming back to life in the context of the dream, or even about the wall collapsing, but the conviction that, if he turns around, the old man will have his face, the son's face, rather than his own.

In the mother's dream, for the first time in a long while, she finds herself back in the children's playground. The son is not playing on the swing, he is sitting on the grass next to her, he is the age he is now. She feels a wave of sadness at the thought of the time that has passed between his birth and this moment, the years contracted to just a few seconds in the dream. Though she does not form the words with her lips, she tells him she wishes that he would stop growing, that he would never become an adult, never know anything of the cruelty of the world, that he would be spared, and the son lowers his eyes and stares accusingly at her belly. Then she remembers she is pregnant with another child, although she has no memory of giving birth, or of having known the child, and her sadness becomes an inconsolable grief.

As for the son, he is not dreaming; he has slipped into a deep sleep, a wholesome oblivion untroubled by the gusts of wind whistling through the roof, the night birds' cries, the rain pounding on the slates and the plastic tarpaulin.

Suddenly, the slender, black tops of the pine trees on the edge of the forest are brutally shaken. A tree falls in the dark heart of the forest, a long wail rises that sends animals scurrying for shelter to their nests, burrows or dens. A momentary flash of lightning illumines the mountain, followed moments later by an explosion, and all three, father, mother and son, wake at the same moment.

The father pulls on a pair of jeans and gets up to close the window shutters banging fiercely in the wind. As he opens the window, a gust of wind brings rain streaming into the room and he must struggle to close the shutters.

Another lightning flash, white as a magnesium flare, rips through the darkness, a deafening peal of thunder rattles the windows and sends the son scurrying from his bed. He appears in the doorway of the parents' room, eyes wide with fear. The mother lifts the blanket next to her, inviting him to take refuge there, and he comes and snuggles in the warm, fragrant imprint left by her body while the father leaves the room.

The rain is now hammering on the roof in a continuous torrent, the slates are clattering in the wind, the tarpaulin inflates and crumples with the rustle of an elytron.

Mother and son stare up at the eaves. They hear the father open the front door when a gust of wind whips away a pile of slates that clatter down the roof. The mother sits up. The wind rushing through the doorway downstairs slips between the cracks in the floorboards. They can smell the intoxicating odour of the night being tossed about by the storm, and when lightning strikes not far from Les Roches, their bones judder in unison with the rocks.

The mother pushes back the sheet and the blanket, swings herself over the edge of the bedframe and is setting her feet on the floor when there comes a long roar from above, as though the storm is drawing strength from its own fury, as though the thick night were mounting an assault on the house, cleaving it from top to bottom, determined to sweep away Les Roches, whose roof is creaking ominously.

The mother grabs the son's arm and pulls him to her just as the roof collapses, taking part of the eaves with it. Debris rains down on the bed and the floor, slates crash to the ground outside the house and mother and child run downstairs, their faces covered in plaster dust.

Rain streams into the vast single room through the wide-open door, soaking the concrete floor and pooling under the table. The mother leads the shivering son to the sofa, and quickly runs to close the door when she sees the father, or rather the motionless figure standing in front of the house, arms dangling by his sides, straight as a ship's mast or a captain standing on the water-beaten deck of a raft about to sink in roiling seas.

It takes her a moment to realize that it really is the father standing there, lashed by the rain, his T-shirt clinging to the bones of his thin, ribbed torso, barefoot amid the splinters of slate. A flash of lightning reveals his ravaged face as he stares up at the roof, blinking back the rain that fills his eyes.

The mother steps outside, and rain washes over her forehead as she follows the father's gaze. On the roof, she sees a shadow like a huge raven's wing flapping in the darkness; it is the tarpaulin, now attached only at one corner, rising and falling like a forge bellows as it is lifted by the wind. When a fresh gust rips it away from the tiles, it slowly rises above their heads before being carried off into the darkness.

She looks back at the father, still standing, frozen, the white of his wide eyes in the darkness. She makes to walk towards him but stops herself and goes back into the house, pulling the door shut. Without letting go of the door handle, she wipes her face with her other hand. The son is lying on the sofa, his legs drawn up to his chest. She goes and sits next to him and, with trembling gestures, wipes his face.

'It's all right,' she says, 'it's all right. It's all right.'

She looks at the hearth, where nothing remains but ash-covered embers, and suddenly becomes aware of how cold the room is. She puts logs in the fireplace, huddles next to the son, covers him with a blanket and hugs him. Soon, flames begin to lick the bark, fanned by the air rushing in. Before long, a fire is furiously crackling in the hearth.

They expect the father to reappear at any moment, but the door remains closed, the father does not return, and as the storm gradually abates, as silence returns to the mountain, troubled only by the mollified whimper of the wind, the boy's head grows heavy, nods, weighs on the mother's arm, and finally he falls asleep, his breathing shallow and regular.

She wakes with a start in the early hours, and before she even opens her eyes, she can sense that the father is in the room. He is sitting at the kitchen table, sleeping, face buried in the crook of his arm on the oilcloth. His hair, which he has not cut since they arrived at Les Roches, is plastered to his head, his clothes are still sodden, his bare feet covered in mud.

The mother sits on the edge of the sofa and drapes the blanket over the child. Warily, she gets up, walks to the front door and peers through one of the windows at the landscape petrified by the ashen light of dawn. She takes one last look at the father, opens the door and goes out.

The smell of mud rises from the meadows pounded by the rain. The ground is littered with slates, rotted battens, scattered tools, leaves and branches blown in by the wind. The tarpaulin, ripped and caught on a thorn bush, lies some thirty metres from the house and the mother sees a hole in the roof, revealing the grimy yellow fibreglass insulation. She walks around the house and sees the remains of the kitchen garden, buried beneath the torrent of mud that has streamed down the slope. As she is about to go back inside, she finds the father standing behind her. He has put on his shoes and changed his T-shirt. A stubbly beard eats into the lower part of his face. His eyes are dark and strangely glassy with exhaustion.

'I'm so sorry,' she says.

'No,' he says. 'No, you're not.'

'We have to go. We can't stay here in these conditions.'

'I'm not going to leave Les Roches in this state.'

'Can't you see it's over? There's nothing left of this place?'

The father brings a cigarette to his lips and furiously bites the filter.

'I don't think you fully understand what all this has cost me,' he says. 'I don't think you fully understand the effort, the sacrifices, the personal commitment involved.'

'Yes, of course I do.'

'I genuinely feel that you're doing everything you can to make our life impossible. To make my life impossible. Couldn't you make a bit of an effort, for fuck's sake? Why can't you take some responsibility? Be a little more positive?'

'I'm about to have a baby, I need medical care. I'm seven months pregnant and I haven't even seen a midwife. It's insane. Don't you understand? It's not about you. I just can't be here.'

'You don't *want* to be here. You never wanted to be here. You never really wanted to give us even a chance, not for one minute. You're doing everything you can to prove that I'm wrong, that things can never be put right.'

He raises the index and middle fingers holding his cigarette towards her, underlining every phrase with a jabbing motion, constantly rocking back and forth on his heels, and she blinks each time his fingers jab.

'You don't think about anything but yourself and the kid,' he roars. 'Did you think I wouldn't notice that you're trying to exclude me from your relationship? And now, you're using the baby as an excuse.'

'It's not an excuse, it's the truth, I think you—'

'Pffft,' he interrupts, slicing the air with his cigarette. 'Don't give me that bullshit. You're being completely selfish. From the minute we got here, you made it clear that you weren't happy with it. Maybe you don't think Les Roches is good enough for you?'

'Can't you see a storm has just blown half the roof off the fucking house?' she says between the ragged sobs engulfing her. 'That for weeks we've done nothing but put up with everything, being up here, you being here with us, your obsession with this place. What do you want me to do? Give birth up here in the mountains?'

'What I want is some respect,' the father bellows in a shower of spittle. 'A little fucking respect and gratitude! What I want is for you to stop bitching and moaning all the time. For you to understand that you're getting exactly what you deserve, no more, no less. That no one but me would give you jack shit, got it?'

The mother takes a step back.

'D'you really think Tony would have wanted anything to do with this kid? That he'd give up his own family for you? Come off it . . . How many guys do you know who'd be prepared to take you in and stay with you knowing you're carrying someone else's child?'

'You're talking as if you gave us the choice to come here,' says the mother. 'But you know perfectly well that this isn't about me, or Tony, or the baby. It's about you, from the beginning it's always been about you, your pride, your vanity, your anger. It's never really been about us getting back together, giving things a chance.'

'Why did you come with me, then?'

'Why did I come with you? Do you really need to ask? I came because I was afraid. I came with you because I'm afraid of you. Even your own son is afraid of you.'

The father lets out a bitter laugh.

'Look at you,' says the mother, wiping her nose with the back of her hand. 'I hardly recognize you. It's like you're being eaten away by something terrible inside, something that is spilling out of you and threatening to destroy everything.'

'Don't talk shit.'

'Let us go. Please. Take us back to town. Take us home. If you won't do it for me, do it for our son.'

The father turns and looks at the house, tosses his cigarette on the ground and grinds it under the toe of his shoe.

'We'll leave when I decide it's time to leave,' he says. 'Now fuck off and leave me in peace. I've work to do.'

Two weeks later, when she feels that enough time has passed and that he is no longer worried about her wanting to leave Les Roches, she decides to take the child and escape.

The father patched up the tarpaulin with tape and did his best to seal up the hole in the roof, but the bedroom he and the mother occupied is still uninhabitable, the plasterboard from the eaves collapsed onto the bed, so he spends his nights on the sofa while mother and son share the other bedroom upstairs.

Every evening she keeps track of his movements downstairs: the light coming up through the chinks in the floorboards when he comes through the door, the dull thud of his footsteps as he goes from sink to table, from table to sofa, the weight of his body slumping onto the velvet seat of the old armchair, the smell of the smoke from the cigarettes he chain-smokes, watching the fire blaze until sleep takes him, even the smell of his sweat, that savage smell he now carries with him everywhere.

She makes the most of being alone with the son to explain that they are leaving that night after the father falls asleep. She says that they will not be taking anything with them. They'll lay out their clothes before pretending to go to bed. She tells the boy that he'll have a few hours to rest, that he'll have to try to sleep because it will be a long walk, and that when she wakes him, they'll have to get dressed in silence, as quietly as possible so as not to wake the father.

She shows him the rucksack she has packed with canteens of water, a packet of biscottes, a couple of extra jumpers, the car key and a flashlight.

She tells the son that they'll have to find the path they took on the way up, that it won't be easy to find in the dark, but it will lead them to the car. Hopefully, the car will start, the mother says, otherwise they'll have to keep walking for as long as it takes to get to the nearest house, probably one of those stark farmhouses they saw along the road on their way up.

What will happen after that, she does not say, but the son can guess. Right now, he needs to rest, gather his strength and, most importantly, when the time comes, remember to make no noise.

That night, they lie next to each other in the son's bedroom, the rucksack and their clothes at the foot of the bed. They stare up at the ceiling, the menacing calm of the house thickened by waiting for the return of the father, who, they imagine, is wandering around Les Roches in the dark. Going about some mysterious business? They don't know, since he has done nothing to repair the roof since the storm, not even gathering up the fallen slates. He simply comes and goes, immured in his bilious silence, mumbling into a beard in which all that can be seen is a glowing cigarette and the whites of his sunken eyes, talking to himself all day long.

The child feels as though he will never be able to get to sleep because the mother's anxiety is palpable, his limbs are tingling with tiny electric shocks, his heart is hammering in his narrow ribcage. But by listening closely to the noises all around, his eyes finally close and he is aware of nothing for a few hours of sleep, during which the mother lies awake next to him, her every sense alert, keenly aware of the presence of the boy next to her and the child she is carrying, of how dependent they are on her, how vulnerable.

When she wakes the son at about two in the morning, pressing a finger to his lips, he thinks he has only just dozed off. He immediately remembers his mother's earlier instructions and feels fear gripping him again.

They stay on the mattress while they get dressed, cautiously leave the room, and stop whenever the floor creaks under their weight. When they reach the top of the steps, the mother signals for the son to wait. She climbs down first, taking care to walk on the outer edges of the steps, until she can see the darkened ground-floor room if she bends down.

The father is sleeping on the chair, head thrown back, mouth open. The mother looks up at the child and gestures for him to follow, guiding his feet as he climbs down to her.

Before he reaches the last few steps, she picks him up and sets him down on the floor next to her and, while she grabs their shoes, the son stands, dazed, at the foot of the stairs, staring at the father, whose face, made gaunter by the flickering flames, is unrecognizable, his right profile completely engulfed by shadows, his Adam's apple more prominent in his throat than usual, as though night is revealing something of his true face: a mass of bones, nerves and cartilaginous protuberances.

The mother touches the son's arm, gestures for him to move towards the door, but as they are crossing the few metres separating the staircase from the entrance, a burnt log noisily implodes in the hearth. She pulls the son to her, puts a hand over his mouth as the father jumps up in the chair. He opens his eyes, mutters something unintelligible, then closes them again and sinks back into sleep. The mother and child stand still, their heartbeats suspended, until they hear a snore come from the father's beard. The mother takes her hand from the son's mouth and pushes him forward. They open the door, but no gust blows into the room; it is a cold, windless night.

Taking infinite precautions, she closes the door behind them, they put on their walking shoes and head off by the crepuscular light of a gibbous moon that makes it possible for them to walk around the house and down the steep path without using the flashlight. When they have gone far enough, she shines the torch beam directly ahead, illuminating black grass, muddy hollows, rocks, resinous tree trunks, and revealing the living, visceral depths of the mountain.

But the mother is finding it hard to walk. She asks the son to slow down as they reach the meadows that were wreathed in mist on the day they first arrived at Les Roches, now lacquered with pale moonlight, with no discernible boundaries. She pauses to catch her breath. Insects appear and disappear in the beam of the flashlight and she stands for a moment, watching spellbound as they flutter frantically, aware of the stillness of the night, its muted rustlings.

She says nothing to the child about the physical discomfort overwhelming her, about the diffuse pain in her belly, nor about the feeling that she is being hurled with him into unfathomable darkness. They carry on walking through damp grass that soaks their shoes and the cuffs of their trousers, through sickly breezes that carry the age-old scent of the rotting undergrowth. As they get closer, the forest before them looms like a shadowy buttress, the tree branches fashioned from blue shadows, the deep, motionless foliage that the beam of the flashlight cannot penetrate.

They follow the rutted track of a grassy path, plunge into the thicker darkness of the forest. The mother stops and sweeps their surroundings with the torch, illuminating indistinguishable trunks, blue-grey ferns. Their memory of the upward journey has faded and darkness makes the topography of the place unrecognizable; they decide to move at random, guided by the gradient of the terrain and the indentations of the path.

'Maman,' says the son.

He points down the path towards the spring under the stump of a dead tree that they drank on the day they made their ascent. They move closer, the flashlight sounding the depths of the crystal-clear water, scaring salamander larvae, which quickly vanish beneath the dead leaves that line the wellspring.

They have just set off again, the child leading the way, when the mother feels a warm liquid pouring out of her, streaming down her thighs. A shudder of fear runs through her, a blow to the sternum that spreads to the tips of her fingers. She stops, falters, wedges the flashlight between her teeth so that her hands are free.

She lifts the flaps of her parka, undoes the top button of her jeans, slides a hand down to her sex then holds it in the beam of the lamp, revealing fingers red with pale blood. The son has turned back to look and she quickly wipes her hand on her jeans as he approaches. She glances up and down the path, trying to funnel the thoughts that flood and pound inside her skull – the routes, the alternatives, the dangers and uncertainties. She feels a wrenching pain in her belly that forces her to hunker down and lean against the muddy verge of the path.

When the child reaches her, she takes his hands in hers and has him crouch down in front of her. She tells him to listen carefully. She says she wishes she could leave the mountain with him, but that she doesn't feel well, that the baby she is carrying doesn't feel well, so they cannot go any further. She tells him it's alright, that sooner or later she will persuade the father that they have to leave the mountain, but right now the boy has to go back to Les Roches to tell him and to ask him for help, since she does not have the strength to make it back unaided.

'Can you find your way back? Did you understand what I'm asking you to do?'

The son nods.

'Alright, go get your father. Take the flashlight and go get your father.'

The child grabs the torch and walks off. Further up the path, he stops and glances back one last time at the crouched body of the mother, now a shadow among shadows, then disappears into the night.

They find her half-conscious where the child left her, the hood of her parka pulled down over her face, her lips blue from the damp chill of the undergrowth.

The father squats down next her and lays a hand on her shoulder. She wakes up, looks at him, looks at the son who is standing in the rut in the path. The man helps her to her feet, puts her arm around his shoulders so that he can take her weight and slips a hand around her waist to support her.

As they head back to Les Roches, moving with laborious, shambling steps, he tells her she was rash and irresponsible in deciding to take the son and leave without a word in the middle of the night, in the state she's in, that she's been reckless, risking not just her own life and that of the unborn child, but the boy's life, if he were left to fend for himself, that she's once again proved that she's irresponsible – once too often – and unworthy of the trust he has placed in her.

'You've only yourself to blame.'

He is speaking into her ear in a low voice, almost a whisper that is inaudible to the son walking on ahead, dazed from exhaustion, a voice mingling disapproval and forbearance as if he were reprimanding a wayward little girl, a sickly child unresponsive to the care lavished on her, and the mother, for her part, says nothing as the father carries her towards Les Roches, in the first blue rays of dawn.

* * *

When they reach the house, he helps her upstairs, undresses her and sits her on the edge of the mattress in the son's bedroom. He wraps a blanket around her shoulders. She sits there as the child watches, shivering, silent, her face in her hands.

The father leaves to fetch a basin of hot water and a flannel that he uses to wipe the mother's face, her neck, the palms of her hands, the brownish blood on her thighs.

'I need to see a doctor,' the mother says again, her voice now emotionless, resigned; a sad fact, expressed only for herself.

'You know that's impossible,' the father says patiently. 'Look at you. We can't leave now.'

He performs every action with painstaking gentleness, rinses the flannel, wrings it out, takes one wrist, lifts the arm, unbends the elbow and the fingers one by one, wipes the pale skin, the muddy lifeline in her palm, then plunges the flannel back into the hot water.

The mother does not say anything, does not move, yielding to the father's ablutions. He tells her to lie on her side, she allows herself to be rocked over onto her hip and he tucks her in with the same care and attention he might adopt when stroking a headstrong animal he has finally forced to submit to his authority, signalling by his caresses and attentions that he forgives her for her snubs.

She closes her eyes and falls asleep, retreating into those comforting depths where the world dissolves, and she feels neither the fingers the father runs over her temple nor the kiss he plants there.

* * *

The father asks the son to leave the mother in peace. He can sleep on the sofa, the father in the armchair. As the child is going to sleep, he warns him: if she is not to lose the baby, the mother needs to stay in bed and take care of herself. The boy also begs the father to take her to a doctor who can treat her and take care of the newborn, but the father shakes his head and tells the child that going back to the town now is out of the question; that the walk could be fatal for both mother and baby.

'She just needs to get her strength back and everything will be fine. Now, go to sleep, we're all together, nothing can happen to us.'

She drifts in and out of a painful half-sleep, leaving the bed only to squat on a bucket the father has left as a chamber pot. She goes from sleep to wakefulness without being sure she can untangle one from the other; the uneasiness even bleeds into her dreams, where the same flights through dark, ominous woods are endlessly repeated, the black earth swamping her steps, the conviction that she is being pursued by something unspeakable, visions of mass graves filled with dead children that she has to search with her bare hands to try to find her own.

When she wakes, she is gripping the sheets to stop herself from a dizzying fall, bathed in sweat, pain boring into her skull. A sense of unreality pours from the dream world into the closed space of the bedroom, melting the lights, distorting shapes and sounds.

The day after they get back to Les Roches, when the son comes to see her and lies next to her, she once again promises that they'll leave as soon as the child is born and she has got her strength back. Then, in the grip of fever and fear, she says no more.

In the days that follow, the father continues to bring her water, bowls of tinned soup that he has to spoon between her lips. He trudges up and down the stairs, changes and washes the sheets, hangs them on a washing line in front of the fireplace where they absorb the smell of ashes, and empties the toilet bucket into the tall grasses in front of the house.

He keeps the son away from the mother, does not allow him to stay with her on the pretext that she needs rest and quiet; on the ground floor, the child is alert to every little sign of the mother's presence in the room, her sighs, the quiet rustle of her body beneath the sheets, her bare footsteps on the floorboards when she moves around.

He also keeps a close eye on the father, desperate to understand and to prevent his dubious perambulations, his comings and goings upstairs, his erratic behaviour, the ominous silence that is broken by wild gesticulations, interjections muttered under his breath, as though he is engaged in a continual inner struggle.

When he asks the boy to go with him into the lean-to to help him bring in firewood, he shows him a huge cardboard box containing packets of powdered baby milk, bottles, nappies, second-hand babygrows, and the son confusedly realizes that the father never had any intention of going back to the town before the child was born, that the provisions shipped up to Les Roches before their arrival were intended for a much longer stay than a single summer, for an indefinite period, months, a year, perhaps more, and that the combination lock he is always careful to set is intended not to prevent an improbable theft, but rather to stop mother and son from going into the lean-to and realizing his intentions before it's time.

A week after their attempt to flee Les Roches, the mother is awakened by the feeling of a shadow unfurling within her.

In the morning, when the father goes up into the bedroom, he finds her motionless, her ashen face thrown back against the pillow, her legs tangled in the blood-soaked sheets, which are already starting to turn black and exude the metallic smell of old iron. Her glassy eyes stare at the grey expanse through the skylight.

Next to her, in the folds of the blanket, lies the baby she delivered in total silence during the night, like a mortally wounded animal gives birth to its offspring, knowing it will not survive; the newborn, a small purple thing, daubed with mucus, is also still and silent.

The father's legs give out under him. He falls to his knees next to the bed, takes the mother's face in his hands, pushes a lock of hair from her forehead and begs her to come back, not to do this to him, not to leave him. He shakes her, presses his lips to hers, his teeth striking hers, as he tries to breathe air that the blocked throat stubbornly refuses.

He vainly pumps his clasped hands on her chest, trying to restart the cold clockwork of the heart. He pulls her to him, hugs her, kisses her rigid temple and caresses her cheek. Over and over, he pleads: I'm sorry, I'm sorry, I'm sorry. He promises that they will go back to town, leave Les Roches, burn it to the ground if need be, if that is what she wants in return for coming back to life, but she staunchly resists his efforts with every fibre of her empty, shrivelled, paltry remains.

He sees the newborn's fist clench in the folds of the blanket, a precarious nest the mother may have fashioned before she died of a massive haemorrhage, bleeding out without a word, in the dark room of this hovel with a gutted roof, in the desolate heart of a mountain.

The face twitches, as the tiny purple mouth, still silent, opens to reveal pink gums and searches for a breast to suckle. The stunned father lays the mother back down on the sheet. He picks up the baby, holds her up before him, his hands trembling, as she stares at him through pale grey eyes, making no sound beyond a barely audible breath.

He pulls his knife from his pocket, flicks out the blade and cuts the umbilical cord, then, groping for a blanket on the floor, he swaddles the child, holds it to his chest and gets to his feet.

When he turns, he sees the son standing in the doorway, staring at the bloody sheet half-covering the mother's body. The father comes out of the room, closing the door behind him, runs a hand over his face to wipe away tears, smearing snot in his beard, then uncovers the infant's mucilaginous head to show the son.

'It's a girl,' he says, his voice ragged with sobs.

* * *

Although premature, the infant survives, nursed on formula by the father, who grips her fiercely to his chest to keep her warm, wraps her in blankets, and sits for endless hours in the armchair by the fire, rocking her with the movement of a broken swing.

He does not give her a name, and the baby, perhaps because she has inherited from the mother the foreknowledge of the threat posed by the father, and the heavy price paid for her existence, scarcely cries and then almost inaudibly when she is hungry, but she sucks at the bottle with a conscientious insatiability, a fierce appetite.

Sometimes, in her sleep, she grabs one of the father's fingers and grips it tightly; the man stares at the small translucent hand with its long nails clutching his finger, racked with sobs, his tears soaked up by the baby's nappy as they fall, and he vows to honour the mother's memory and care for her.

Down below, the son is devastated. He sits on the bottom step of the stairs, watching for some sign from the mother that would belie the vision of her body wrapped in crimson sheets, but a lugubrious silence hangs over the house, broken by the father now and then as though he is carrying on a conversation he left off earlier, alternately addressing the son, the mother, himself, the ghost of his own father.

Eventually, the baby's silence begins to weigh on the father like an accusation, a rebuke.

The mouse-grey eyes stare at him unblinking.

'What do you want from me?' he suddenly roars. 'Can't you be normal, like any other fucking baby?'

The newborn wriggles in his hands but does not cry, and the father sets down the swaddled child so he can avoid her gaze and storms out, slamming the door so hard behind him that the doorframe cracks.

Night and day, the presence of the mother's body in the upstairs room weighs upon them like a curse.

If he's left her up there, thinks the son, does that mean that, somehow, she's still alive? Does she not need anything? How does she spend her days and nights? Surely she must think that he's abandoned her, surely she must mourn for the child who has been taken from her?

In the father's absence, the son ventures upstairs, but as soon as he reaches the landing, he is struck by an acrid smell that is instantly recognizable. The father has stopped up the gap under the door with rags and towels; only the keyhole allows a faint ray of sunlight that is instantly blocked by a tiny body of metallic blue. Emerging from the keyhole the son sees a blowfly – 'a carrion fly,' as his mother used to say, when a blowfly that had probably hatched in a rubbish bin flew into the kitchen of the cramped terraced house and banged against the windows. It falls onto its back on the floor, buzzing in small circles for a moment before coming to rest. Images flood the boy's mind of carcasses he has seen in the woods – the tattered fur and bloated, barely-recognizable bodies of animals teeming with vermin – and he quickly runs back down the stairs.

* * *

Now they eat only food from tins whose contents the father does not bother to heat before slopping onto already dirty plates. The dishes pile up amid the cans full of cigarette butts, on the spattered oilcloth littered with rubbish. The father barely touches his food, he sits facing the son – who forces himself to eat out of fear of being punished – chain-smoking as his body moves in tics and convulsive jerks.

His eyes are ringed with deep, dark circles, his face is even more terrifyingly gaunt. He walks with stooped shoulders and juddering movements, the glowing tips of his cigarettes casting a reddish glow on his grimy brown face.

He now spends long hours sitting on a chair facing the front door, the revolver resting in his lap. With the tip of his knife, he cuts away the dead, calloused skin on his hands, extracts splinters from his fingers, wiping the pus from the reopened wounds on his trousers.

'They'll come,' he says to the son. 'Sooner or later, they'll come.'

'Who?' say the child.

The father gives a contemptuous shrug.

'The public works officer. Someone from the town council. Maybe even that fucker Tony.'

One night, the generator behind the stone wall lets out a series of coughs and splutters followed by mechanical clangs; the naked bulb hanging from the ceiling of the single ground-floor room flickers and goes out, plunging Les Roches into darkness. In the hearth, the embers are covered with ash.

The father goes to check the generator. Acrid smoke billows from the lean-to, which he has to air out before he can set foot inside. Worried by the smell, the son comes to join him, but does not cross the threshold. Hunkered down, with the flashlight gripped between his teeth, the father sees that the generator, from which he removed the cut-off switch to increase the power supply, has burned out and is beyond repair.

The cartilage in his knees cracks as he puts a hand on his thigh to stand up. He sucks his teeth, staring at the smoking apparatus. As he is about to leave, he spots a sledgehammer, its handle is resting against the wall. He sets the torch down on a pile of logs, grabs the hammer, runs back and batters the generator over and over, and with every blow a dry rattle emerges from his scrawny chest and joins the shriek of rending metal.

He smashes up the crankcase, bursts the tank which spills out over the ground, petrol sprays into his face, the sledgehammer cracks the cylinder head, snaps the drive belt. The father stops, panting, only when the heart of the machine has been destroyed, obliterated. Suddenly, he seems to calm again, drops the hammer in the dust at his feet and picks up the torch before leaving. At the first blow of the sledgehammer, the son ran into the house and, hugging his baby sister to him, sought refuge in a shadowy corner under the stairs.

A few days later, the father is sitting facing the boy at what is supposed to be dinner time. The flashlight hanging from a joist by a piece of string swings limply in the breeze as it casts a pool of white light over their foreheads. The father has set the revolver on the table in front of him and watches as the son picks up small forkfuls of food that he struggles to chew. The child's face is gaunt now, the light from the lamp accentuates the hollow of his cheeks. He constantly has to pull his trousers over his hips. He no longer washes himself; his hair, which has grown since their arrival at Les Roches, is greasy and matted; the folds of his neck, his arms and wrists are caked with grime. The father grabs the butt of the gun and aims at the boy.

The son puts down his fork and sits motionless, staring wide-eyed at the barrel of the gun which is shaking so violently that the father has to use his left hand to steady it. Suddenly the father's strength is drained, his arms fall limp, his face contorts into a ghastly rictus and he lets out a long, desperate roar before sweeping his arm across the table, sending plates, cutlery and the rotting remains of food crashing to the floor. He empties the cylinder chambers of the three bullets he loaded earlier – one for the son, one for the baby, one for himself – then gets up and goes to stow the gun in the drawer of the old china cabinet in the lean-to.

Before long, the mother's remains fill the house with the stench of a slaughterhouse. Blowflies have spread to the ground floor; they settle on the windows and the joists, flying in droning battalions and crashing into the flashlight, covering it with shit.

Only now does the father decide to bury her.

He gathers up a mass of planks, battens and laths from the lean-to and the ruins of the outbuildings. He piles them up in front of the house, saws and planes them, and on a pair of trestles, he fashions a crude rectangular box composed of various colours and types of wood. Patiently, he sands the box, his face and forearms covered in sawdust, the air filled with the smell of powdery wood, but it is only when he fits a lid that the son realizes that he has built a coffin for the mother.

He wraps the baby in thick blankets and tells the son to follow him to the lean-to, where he grabs a pickaxe and a shovel and hands one of them to the boy.

They walk through a fog that shrouds the world for more than ten metres around, towards a shadow that turns out to be a blackthorn tree with gnarled branches, blue with parmelia and purple berries, and at its foot the father places the sleeping baby.

He walks around the tree, pushing the blade of the shovel into the earth in several places until he finds a patch of loose soil, then marks out a rectangle about two metres by eighty centimetres and begins to dig.

A light rain begins to fall again, but the son stands, uncovered, next to the pit, and his clothes are quickly soaked. He watches as the father rips out clods of black earth and sets them on the rim, where amputated pieces of earthworm writhe at the edges.

The man digs with the same stubborn persistence he had when preparing the ground for the kitchen garden, but this time there is no anger, no fury; he digs with desolate, forlorn, determined obstinacy, staring at the bottom of the hole which grows deeper, darker and more symmetrical with each blow of the pickaxe.

He pays no heed to the son or the newborn baby dozing in the shelter of the bluish blackthorn branches, from which ripe fruit falls, is caught in the folds of the blankets, and rolls onto the baby's downy forehead.

After hours of toiling with the pickaxe, when the father reaches the layer of stone that halts the axe's progress, the grave comes up to his thigh. Placing his hands on the edge, he hauls himself out and sprawls on his back.

'I can't do any more. I can't dig any deeper,' he says, though the son does not know whether the statement was addressed to him.

He lies next to the pit, sickly and scrawny, his face haggard, his eyes sunken, as though he has been drained of all substance and only bones remain.

His muddy hands still clutch the handle of the pickaxe resting on his chest. Swathes of mist dissolve against the sky, revealing soaring heights of chalcedony blue across which the streamlined shape of a plane is slowly moving. Though no sound reaches their ears, the very sight of the plane is an unprecedented irruption of a parallel reality, the remanence of the world they left when they came to Les Roches and which no longer seemed to exist.

They follow the path of the shimmering, surreal, tubular form of the fuselage as it appears and disappears, cleaving the cumulus clouds before disappearing behind the mountain ridge, leaving only a trail of condensation in its wake that quickly fades into azure.

Leaning on the handle of the pickaxe, the father gets up, drops the tool and walks away.

'Wait here,' he says to the son without turning back.

Alone in front of the grave, the boy cannot help but step closer so he can see the bottom, the ochre puddle that has formed there, which reflects his stooped silhouette, framed against the blue sky.

Behind him, the newborn is awake now and raises her hands towards the blurred shadows of the branches, whose rustle she tries to catch. The boy sits down beside her and, as she gulps air with her mouth, he gently brings his little finger to her lips. The infant soothes herself, sucking on the first phalanx.

They rest there in the bittersweet perfume of trampled sloes that litter the ground, looking at each other for a long time, seeming to recognize each other or to recognize in one another the persistence of the mother, and, for a suspended moment, the mountain forms a cosy and auspicious nest around them.

Then the father reappears.

He has balanced the coffin on the wheelbarrow and strapped it in place. The boy gets up and watches as he lurches towards them. When the wheel encounters a stone, the coffin threatens to tip, sometimes left, sometimes right. When he reaches the grave, the father undoes the straps and, in a difficult manoeuvre, lowers one end of the coffin to the ground while holding up the other end. He sets it down next to the grave and collapses. The smell of ripe sloe mingles with the sweet, acidic scent of the coffin's mismatched timbers. The father kneels, hands on the ground, and retches violently until only a trickle of yellow bile escapes his lips and drips onto the grass.

Panting for breath, he wipes his mouth, climbs down into the grave and orders the son to push the coffin towards him. At first, the child cannot move a muscle, but the father points an imperious hand and long, dirty fingernails at the coffin. The son obeys, pushes with all his might and slides it across the slippery grass to the muddy edge of the grave, where he loses his footing. As the coffin tips over, he feels the stiff weight of the mother's body banging against the wooden side. The father grabs a corner, pulls it towards him, struggling to bear the weight before it slips from him and falls to the bottom of the grave, sending up a spray of muddy water that dashes his face.

He clambers out of the hole, grabs the shovel again and plunges it into the sodden earth, but the son jumps forward and stands between him and the mother's body, screaming at the top of his lungs for him to leave her alone, to get away from her. Tells the father that he hates him, wishes he was the one in this grave, in this box. With all his strength, he pounds his fists on the father's stomach, chest and arms, and the father calmly stands, weary or determined, and takes the blows which are deadened by his sodden clothes. In the end, the son tires himself out and has nothing left to flay the father with but eyes filled with tears, fury and despair.

'Hate me all you like,' the father says, 'but it's too late. What's in the box, in that pit, that's not her anymore. It's everything except her.'

Again, he thrusts the blade into the pile of earth, tosses the first shovelful of dirt into the shadowy pit where it lands on the wooden lid with the sound of falling rocks, and the son, now helpless, watches as he fills the grave, burying the mother's body beneath the mineral darkness of the mountain's belly.

And when the father has filled the hole, when the sole remaining vestige of the mother's existence is a rectangle of disturbed earth over which the meadow will quickly reassert itself, without so much as a crucifix cobbled together from a couple of twigs and planted at an angle on the black mound to mark its location, the father lights a cigarette and says:

'Let's go home.'

He drags his baleful carcass towards Les Roches, and the son, whose tears have all dried up, gathers his sister in his arms, takes one last look at the grave and falls into step.

Somehow, as though life here could carry on without the mother, as though he expects the son to take on the same role he played with his old man, the father goes back to doing the same things that were once part of daily life at Les Roches – before their world was shattered into pieces – that monotonous routine, that trance, those days devoid of anything, filled with the magnetic presence of the mountain.

He drags from the house the mattress and sheets, stained black like a funeral shroud, douses them with petrol and sets them alight. Oily smoke fills Les Roches as the burning mattress reveals the springs and bubbling foam of its entrails. He stands next to the inferno, feeding the blaze with sprays of petrol, his face completely expressionless, his eyes fixed on the heart of the flames, and when, finally, he turns away, it is to go and split logs and store them in the lean-to.

There follow days of slow autumnal drift, murky light, hazy hours, dawn following dusk in an infinite variation of monochrome beneath a constant drizzle, the mountain mantled every morning in a shroud of mist.

The son withdraws, and now spends his time with the newborn. He feeds her, changes her, cradles her, anticipating her every need so he can ward off the father, who watches from the sidelines, his expression sometimes vacant, as though his body is present but empty, sometimes wild-eyed.

Every day, the boy goes back to visit the mother's grave, where rain and damp nights have compacted the mound. Already, the pale shoots are appearing on the tilled earth. The son brings stones that the father removed to create the kitchen garden, and arranges them over the grave, a pitiful tomb on which he lays armfuls of late wildflowers, thistles, asters and foxgloves whose dry corollas rustle softly when breezes drift through the meadow.

Just as he saw the mother do, he surreptitiously puts together a little bundle, a child's backpack that he hides under the sofa when the father's back is turned: a few tins of food, some baby formula, a flashlight, a survival blanket, charms from an old bracelet, one of the mother's T-shirts that still has her smell. And he waits, as paralyzed by the father's volatile presence as by the prospect that he, in turn, will fail, but a few weeks after the mother has been laid to rest, when he sees the man loading plastic containers into the wheelbarrow to fetch water, the child knows that he must seize this opportunity.

He listens to the sound of plastic against metal, the steady clatter of the wheel as the man pushes it down the path lined with nettles, hawking up phlegm and spitting on the verge, and when the sounds fade, the child jumps down to the sofa, lies on the concrete floor and pulls out all the things he has hidden there, stuffing them into a backpack.

He goes out of the house and over to the lean-to. Since they first arrived at Les Roches, he has watched the father open the combination lock, hiding the small notched wheels beneath the pad of his thumb as he turns them, then leaving the lock hanging on the bolt, glinting coldly in the light. The son has carefully memorized the first two numbers he has glimpsed as the wheels were turned. Now, he feverishly searches for the last two combinations, looking over his shoulder lest the father reappear at any moment, but the lock resists the efforts of his fingers numbed by fear – there is no Open Sesame, the little wheels spin vainly on their pivot.

Seeing the pickaxe the father used to dig the mother's grave lying in the grass, the son drags it to the lean-to, tries to raise it above his head, but the axe is too heavy and falls at his feet, the pick sinking into the soft earth. He picks it up again, gripping it higher, wedging the handle against his pelvic bone, and tries several times to hit the lock. Still the pickaxe strays from its true course, scratches the wooden door, barely grazing the lock. The boy's arms are shaking from his efforts, he is panting for breath. For a moment, he leaves the tool resting at his feet, ready to give up, then raises it again, and, with a howl of rage, brings it down with all his strength. This time the sharp pick hits the bolt, which becomes detached from the door.

The son drops the pick and grabs the bolt with both hands. Placing one foot flat on the door, he heaves until the bolt comes away and he is sent sprawling backwards. He jumps to his feet, rushes into the lean-to and empties the contents of the old china cabinet at his feet. The three bullets roll across the floor amid a jumble of objects, but the revolver is not among them. The child picks them up, studies them in the palm of his hand and is about to give up when he sees the grubby piece of cloth protruding from one of the upper shelves. He slips the bullets into a pocket, hauls himself up, placing one foot in the empty space left by a drawer, and using every ounce of strength, heaves himself up until his fingertips can touch the cloth. The bundle clatters to the floor, revealing the revolver, which now lies in the dust, heavy and matte grey. The son climbs down, picks up the weapon and heads back into the house.

The newborn has woken up; she is nestled in the little crib he made from an apple crate. She gazes at him with placid eyes as he stuffs the revolver into the rucksack, heaving a sigh only when he wraps her in a blanket and takes her in his arms. He is heading for the door, about to leave, when he turns to contemplate the obscene chaos of the vast room. He retraces his steps, takes a blazing log from the hearth and puts it on the sofa, wedged between the seat cushions. He waits until the flames serenely rise and lick the threadbare velvet with a gentle hiss, then throws on handfuls of the kindling that the father piled up next to the hearth.

He moves as quickly as the burdens of baby and rucksack allow, not towards the path he took with the mother, where he might bump into the father, but over the meadows, towards the forest of red larches. Only when he reaches the edge of the wood does he turn back to Les Roches to see the blaze. All he can see is a glowing halo in the waning light, so bright that it looks as though the fire has consumed the sky itself. A tall column of black smoke is drifting westwards.

The child stands frozen, the incandescent halo reflected in his black pupil. What he cannot see from his vantage point, he can imagine: flames licking the beams and battens, spreading upstairs in a thunderous crackle, feverishly devouring the partition walls and the roof, the father, seeing the conflagration as he is heading home, abandoning the wheelbarrow filled with canisters of water and running to Les Roches. Will he fall to his knees, will he brave the flames and search through the rubble for the bodies of his son and the newborn?

The boy steps into the dappled shade of the forest. He makes his way through the undergrowth, struggling to carry his sister who has fallen asleep. His muscles, once tensed with fear, are now quivering. As the last light fades, he forks towards the old walnut tree and, reaching it, he lays the baby on the ground next to the hollow in the roots. He drags a dead branch towards the opening, leaving it within easy reach, and pushes the rucksack into the hollow before creeping in, carrying the baby, and pulling the branch over to hide the entrance. In the confined space, he has just enough room to take the canteen, the feeding bottle and the formula from the rucksack, prepare the bottle and feed the baby. His sister suckles intently, running her little fingers over his face. The boy is suddenly overwhelmed by exhaustion. The light beneath the trees is fading, a damp chill is rising, filled with the perfumes of the night, brackish water holes, stumps and rancid ferns. He takes his mother's T-shirt from the rucksack, buries his face in it and inhales her smell.

The father's voice comes to him in his sleep. He wakes with a jolt, startling his sister. Through the branch that covers the hole, the boy can dimly make out the forest engulfed in algid gloom. The condensed breath of their conjoined bodies fills the hollow with moist air and an acrid stench. The boy feels the baby's full nappy and pulls a face.

For a moment, he thinks that he has dreamed the father's voice and is about to turn on the flashlight when the voice rings out again, calling his name, so close at hand it makes him flinch. The top of his head hits the mud wall which showers earth over his shoulders. The son holds his breath; the sound of footsteps, the rustle of ferns, trampled branches, guttural breath.

A torch beam slices through the undergrowth, lingers on them, its light splintered by the branch concealing them; still, the son holds his breath and the beam moves on, the father calls to him again in a desperate, pleading tone the child does not recognize. Silently he implores his sister to be quiet and she placidly returns his gaze, her nostrils barely flaring with her breath.

The father's footsteps grow more distant. Still the son waits for minutes that seem interminable until all he can hear is the now familiar murmur of the forest. He pushes aside the covering at the entrance to the hollow, pokes his head out and surveys the area and, seeing no sign of the father, clambers out, hugging the baby to his chest, retrieves the rucksack and runs blindly through the forest.

He heads towards the stream. As he approaches, the roaring water drowns out his footsteps. The current shines with glints of mercury and twists like a languid grass snake between the stones. Here the son no longer needs the flashlight. He pauses on the bank, lays his sister in the blanket on a large flat rock. The stream enfolds them in a damp chill that makes him shiver. He takes off the baby's cloth nappy, which he uses to clean her before trying to rinse it in icy water that numbs his fingers, until he realizes he has no way to dry it and allows the current to carry the terrycloth away.

Reaching into the rucksack, he takes out the mother's T-shirt, knots it around the baby's hips and is wrapping her in the blanket when, out of the corner of his eye, he glimpses a hulking shadow and stops. A bear shambles towards them, calmly emerging from the undergrowth, breathing heavily. The moonlight lends its thick brown fur a ghostly bluish lustre. The terrified boy crouches over his sister and does not move. The bear comes to the stream, where, for a long time, it drinks. When it raises its head, water dribbles from its mouth. The bear shakes itself and yawns, revealing sharp teeth set into its powerful jaws, then wades into the stream. The child tries to make himself as small as possible, his petrified body huddled over the baby. He hears the bear approaching, he breathes in the smell of wet fur, which is both animal and vegetal, as though the bear's pelt has preserved the smell of moss from the undergrowth. The animal stops close by, less than two metres away, and sniffs him. The boy can feel its ragged breath on the back of his neck, he tilts his head towards it slightly and catches a glimpse of one of its huge paws on the rock, the sodden fur, the curved claws. Then the bear seems to lose interest in the child, turns and heads downstream with a majestic gait. For a long time, the boy remains motionless, knees and elbows aching from the pressure of the rock, and when, finally, he dares to stand, all that remains of the bear's presence is a grey paw print on the stone.

The yellow halo of the flashlight bounces off the ground as he runs, without the least idea of which direction he has taken. Around him, the forest has become darker, denser. When he stops, his every sense alert, he hears the ambient murmur made up of a thousand tiny sounds: the quiver of trees in the wind, the constant fall of etiolated leaves, the talons of nocturnal raptors clawing at the bark of the branches on which they perch, hawk-eyed watchers.

The baby in the son's arms starts to fret and whimper. They are gripped by hunger and thirst. He knows that soon he will have to stop again, but he walks on, choosing to take the upward slope. After a difficult trek, he comes to an area of flat ground and finds himself forced to walk along the edge of a cliff where the roots of stunted pine trees grow into the rockface. The beam of the flashlight moves across the gnarled trunks, the rocks oozing with the humidity of night, blackened with the trickles of sap that they disgorge, then the halo of light is sucked into a large hollow partially covered by vegetation.

The son stops, stares into the murky depths, wonders whether this is an old mineshaft like the one he discovered during his wanderings, or whether it is the bear's den. His fear is mitigated by sheer exhaustion; this gaping maw in the body of the mountain seems less terrifying than the prospect of the father finding them. He ventures far into the thick darkness of the hollow, passes through a low tunnel that would force an adult to stoop and comes to a cave whose vaulted roof rises almost three metres. The air smells like a cold, damp crypt.

Holding his sister close, the boy moves the beam of the torch over the limestone concretions that extend from the top to the floor of the cave, where it plunges further into the secret forking depths. His eye is caught by curious marks on the flat grey wall. He steps closer and studies the remains of a cave painting depicting an animal with slender legs, its skull topped with intricately carved antlers that spread like roots; the beast is being pursued by three human figures. Two are armed with spears, the third has none, but there is a dark line stuck into the creature's flank.

The son cannot know that, since it was traced here with iron oxide and chalk in the dawn of time, no human eye has looked upon this cave painting. He stands, fascinated by this thing that has appeared in the beam of the flashlight; he can almost hear the clatter of hooves on hard ground and the breathless panting of the men, feel the fear of the prey and the excitement of the hunters.

Eventually, he walks away because his head is spinning and he huddles against a wall. The torchlight on the newborn's face shows that her skin is pale, her lips blue. The boy rubs her as the mother often did to warm him up. He clasps her tiny hands in his, brings them to his mouth and breathes warm air from his lungs. When the sister's colour returns, he opens his parka jacket and lays her against his chest, unfolds the survival blanket and wraps it around his shoulders. He takes a tin of tuna from the rucksack, pierces the lid and drinks the juice. He eats the flaky tuna, taking time to chew it properly. He also eats some of the shortbread biscuits his mother used to soak in hot milk and give him for breakfast, and suddenly he is struck by a feeling of unfathomable loneliness, by the thought of having forever lost his mother.

His mind is flooded by images of her benevolent presence, her loving gestures, and then images of the body glimpsed through the door of the upstairs room at Les Roches, of the muddy hole in the earth, of the rudimentary coffin crudely cobbled together by the father. And if he does not weep, it is because there is a fierce hatred welling inside him, a hatred that pounds through his heart and his temples, radiates out to his limbs. Once again, he hears his name, bellowed by the father somewhere in the forest, deeper now, more ghostly, as though coming from the mountain itself. The son delves into the rucksack, takes out the revolver and, with clumsy gestures, loads the three bullets. The biddable weapon clicks and closes in the child's hands. The flaps of his parka are folded over the baby. The son switches off the flashlight, sits, motionless, gripping the gun, his eyes staring into the utter darkness of the cave.

Before day breaks, the night is ripped by bolts of lightning that reveal great black rolling clouds about to lash the earth. A heavy downpour, briefly impeded by the lush treetops, pierces the dense foliage and pummels the ground.

The boy has slept only intermittently, startled by the slightest sound. To him, the night felt like a constant shifting between wakefulness and dream, evocations of the mother, memories of hunting in the woods which his mind may have created out of whole cloth or which may be the memories of others before him, he does not know.

He gets up, urinates against the wall, fills the canteen with the rain dripping from the rock at the entrance to the cave. He tries to feed his sister some of the remaining formula, but she stubbornly turns her head away. She looks frail, lethargic and numb with cold. He pulls the blanket tighter, pulls down his hood and leaves their refuge.

The undergrowth is covered in a thick mist. The trees are little more than charcoal strokes whose topmost branches are invisible. The boy looks around, unable to get his bearings. Around him, the rain patters, his feet slip on the carpet of dead leaves, as though the mountain were oozing this rust-coloured humus. The ground falls steeply and several times he falls on his behind and has to pull himself up by clinging to the wet bark of the trees. He walks for a long time, forcing himself to be cautious, with the feeling that the forest is growing, distorting and endlessly regenerating.

It is then that he sees the father, or rather recognizes the father's profile at the bottom of a slope, barely distinguishable through the fog, a vertical yet broken shadow moving between the trees. The son lies down on his back behind a fallen trunk, focusing his attention on the deadened sound of the father's progress. He props himself up on one elbow to peer over the trunk, but his view is blocked by the trees and the mist. He lies, frozen, amid the smell of rotting wood and humus, rain falling on his face, his sister's tiny, motionless body pressed against his chest.

After a long wait, and hearing nothing but the patter of the rain, he warily gets to his feet and retraces his steps. Cradling the newborn with one hand, he uses the other to climb back up the slope he has come down, levering himself up using stones, roots and fallen branches. From behind him comes the sound of running footsteps and, when he reaches the top of the escarpment, the son turns to look.

The man is some fifteen metres below, and although he cannot quite make out the face, the boy would swear that he is looking straight up at him. Unmoving, they observe one another; the father does not speak, does not even call his name. Perhaps he has used up all his words. He does not make the slightest move, as though trying to accustom the child to the sight of him, to his presence, or perhaps gauging the distance between him and the child. Slowly, he raises both hands in a sign of peace, then takes a step towards the son, who immediately takes off at full speed. The father races up the steep slope after him, trips, gets to his feet and resumes his difficult climb.

All around the child, the undergrowth flashes past, nebulous, surreal, though now framed by the harsh white light of day. He runs in a straight line, disoriented, swerving here and there to take advantage of gaps in the undergrowth, or to avoid fallen trees. He stops to look around him, panting for breath, exhausted by his running and the weight of his sister, which makes his arms and his back ache. He knows he cannot carry on much longer, that the father – or the creature transformed by Les Roches, the thing that once claimed the right to be his father – with his long, swift strides will eventually catch him in the impenetrable heart of the forest from which there is no escape. Yet the son carries on walking, urged on by despair and by the ageless, primal fear of prey being tirelessly hounded by the hunter.

Trying to follow the daylight, he starts down a gentle slope and slows his pace. He is encircled by tall trees whose smooth white bark flecked with black is peeling away in long coils, as though their growth had been achieved by constantly sloughing off skin. Bright yellow leaves quiver on the branches. As he walks through the trees, the son sees old wounds left by a blade, over which the regenerated bark has formed long, pale suppurating scars. Once, they haemorrhaged sap which streamed down their trunks, where it has been frozen by the years into dark bilious trails. Some of the birch trees are dead; all that remains is a bare trunk, green with moss, raised to the sky. Others have collapsed under their own weight, broken where they were weakened by the axe blows, and lie aslant, held up by the branches of adjacent trees or sprawled on the ground. The grove of silver birches reminds the child of a huge ossuary, of illustrations seen in books depicting the carcasses of prehistoric animals of which little remains beyond a pair of tusks or bleached white ribs. Huge bunches of mistletoe, heavy with translucent berries, cast spectral shadows over the branches.

The wind rises and the mist unravels, revealing a leaden sky across which a flock of greylag geese is passing low, heralded by their cries. The son looks up at them, his face dripping sweat and rain. He kneels and sets his sister down, taking care to pull the survival blanket from over her face. The newborn's eyes are closed, her forehead is burning, her breathing quick and shallow. A sob quivers in the boy's chest, but he instantly stifles it. When he gets to his feet, she opens her eyes again. The two children look at each other, and the boy makes her a silent promise before moving off and disappearing from her sight. Drawing on her last reserves of strength, the baby starts to cry, and her voice rises in a fierce, hysterical, desperate wail that pierces the sepulchral silence of the birch grove.

The man emerges, stops dead, struck to the core by the sight of the birch trees. The baby's cries have led him to her. He sees her lying in the glittering gold of the survival blanket which crinkles between the little fists grabbing and tugging at it. The rain has abated, but a fine drizzle still settles on the soil. Without so much as a glance at the wounded trunks of the birch trees, the man closes the space that separates them with a curious sluggishness, pulling his feet from the mud at every step. He moves jerkily, like a stick insect, so slowly that it seems as though at any moment the mountain might open up and swallow him, and when he finally reaches the newborn, he trembles in his sodden clothes and hangs his head, as though standing at the foot of his own grave.

He does not hear the son creep from the undergrowth where he has been lying in wait, nor does he hear him walk towards him, but he hears the click of the hammer as the son cocks the gun behind him. He lifts his head without surprise, slowly turns and stares, with wild, weary eyes, at the barrel aimed at his chest. The boy grips the gun with both hands, he does not blink, his eyes glitter with an old, familiar rage, too long suppressed.

The father, whose spidery fingers are caked black with dirt and grime, fumbles in his pockets and, with tremulous gestures, raises a crumpled cigarette to his lips.